THE HOUSE OF STONES

Kathryn Rankin Covington

Birch Tree Press

ISBN: 978-1-7371574-8-9

Cover design by Nicole Warrington

Printed in the United States of America

This book is dedicated to the family
who blazed the trail
and taught us to walk
with our heads held high.

This book is dedicated especially
to my parents,
Sharon and Dan.

CHAPTER ONE

Salt burned Anya's cheek as she paddled the canoe across the bay. She clenched her teeth, determined not to cry. There was work to be done.

Wind whipped through the air as dusk began to settle, but she could still see the island in the distance; surely the wise woman would give her a torch to light her way back. In her head, the music of the harp rang clear, propelling her onward.

Cillian had played in church this past Sunday and Anya had begged her mother to come hear him, sure that the music he played would lift her spirits. Her father had insisted that her mother was too ill to come and must stay in bed. Instead, Joseph had called the widow Mariloup to come and sit with her mother while Anya and he attended church. Cillian had caught her eye as he played and smiled that half smile that struck lightening through her veins. They had met for a few words after the service, Cillian grasping her hand in the middle of the village, asking to see her, to meet her, anywhere, in the grove. But Anya wouldn't go anywhere until she had fetched the herbs for her mother from the Island.

Anya breathed the sea air deeply.

The doctor had been by this morning. His news was dire. Mariloup sat there dabbing at dry cheeks with an embroidered handkerchief, her mother's sewing was so much finer. Joseph heard the news stone-faced. When the doctor finished with his proclamation, the color drained from Joseph's chiseled cheekbones and he took himself out the door. Mariloup arose, announcing that she would "fix a plate for the poor man," and Anya took her place at the bedside.

"What can I do, Mama?" she asked, dipping a bit of cloth in the pail of cool water and patting her mother's forehead.

Her mother smiled weakly. "Find the mantle. In the bureau. Make sure it's clean."

Anya shook her head. "I can do more," she said, swallowing hard. Liora gave a weak smile to her daughter.

"You can do anything, Anya. I know. You can make your life beautiful."

"But for you, Mama," Anya had insisted, squeezing her mother's hand. "What can I do now? For you?"

Liora swallowed with difficulty and Anya brought the teacup to her mother's lips. Liora sipped dutifully and motioned for Anya to lie back onto the bed next to her.

"Go to my sister," Liora had said. "On the Island. Tell her what the doctor said." Anya nodded. "But only

2

when the weather is fine," Liora said. "You are young, but the wind will take you if you aren't careful."

"Your mother needs rest." Mariloup's voice was saccharine and it took every fiber in Anya's body not to speak back. Ignoring Mariloup, she turned to her mother. "The wind is gentle today. I'll go after supper."

"Thank you," she said. Liora nodded and seemed to rest, but not before Anya saw the urgency that lay in her sunken blue eyes.

Anya clenched her teeth at the memory of the morning. The waves whipped, but Anya's strong arms held the oars firmly. The trees were beginning to take shape before her as she navigated the canoe into the hidden cove. Not many could safely get to the island, but she knew the secrets of the wind. As she rowed into the hidden inlet, she could smell the smoke burning from the chimney of the house buried in the woods.

CHAPTER TWO

Anya walked down the sandy path laden with fallen pine needles. No carts or horses ever came to this island; a boat large enough to transport them could never dock. She dragged her canoe up upon the rocky beach as her mother had taught, far enough ashore and protected under the tree grove so as not to be taken back by the waters. Today, Anya did not stop to look at the stones for their beauty and for their secrets. There wasn't time.

The golden autumn leaves of the birches fluttered down upon her head as she hurried through the canopy of trees. The breeze was kinder in the forest.

Anya knew that when the path seemed to stop at the fallen aspen tree, she must carefully pick her way among the crumbling ferns until she reached the jasper stone. Absently, Anya touched the stone and then touched her forehead, heart, and belly, whispering "Wisdom, Love, Creativity" with each touch. A glance at the darkening sky sent her hurrying onward without stopping to feel the blessings.

Airmed was waiting at the threshold. Even in her hurry, the sight of the stone house sparkling in the twilight took Anya's breath away. Granite, jasper, ancient coral, agate and basalt stones larger than wagon wheels shimmered, beckoning her closer. Joseph had asked Liora countless times why, if the sisters owned a home of such value, why they would not sell the stones and make life easier for them all. But Liora had always shaken her head. "A home can only be built on a bedrock of love. Otherwise it is worth nothing." Once, Anya had been brave enough to ask her mother about the stones. Her mother looked at her and said only "The stones contain all that we need. If we sold them for money, they would be worthless. That stone house is our family." Liora had reached up to touch the double strand of pearls that always graced her neck and touched her daughter's hand. "When you are of age, you and I will go to the Island and Airmed and I will show you."

Well, Anya was on the Island now and of age enough. It was time for the mystery to be over. If the stones were the family, the stones could jolly well help.

"The stones will help your mother." Anya whipped her head toward the figure in the door. "Come." Her aunt Airmed gestured toward the door. "I have already ground them."

CHAPTER THREE

Airmed clasped Anya's hand in both of her own and stared into her aqua eyes. "Eilidh," she whispered.

"Anya," the younger woman answered firmly.

Airmed scoffed. "That's your father's doing. Your mother blessed you with the shining light of the Goddess when you were born. That is what the name of Eilidh means. It was your father who insisted on Anglicizing it." Airmed reached across to touch a burgundy curl that the wind had blown loose, smiling proudly. "You are strong. You were one with the wind today. I saw you coming across the waters."

Anya met her aunt's gaze. "My mother is sick. The doctor says there is nothing he can do. But I know you can. If you would just consent to sell some of these stones, we could pay for a better doctor. From Montreal."

Airmed searched the younger woman's face and sighed. Leading her over the threshold, she gestured to a hand-carved chair. "Sit, Eilidh." Passing her a cup of steaming tea, she instructed, "Stir counterclockwise. Rid yourself of these false notions."

"But - "

"No buts, child. A doctor from Montreal may well know better than the fool treating your mother. But he will be too late to help."

Tears sprang to Anya's eyes and she swallowed hard to push them back. "Will you come, Aunt Airmed?"

"Sip the tea," Airmed commanded. "I cannot. You know that. But I will send you with what you need. What your mother needs." Airmed locked eyes with her niece until Anya had dutifully stirred and sipped the tea. "Keep drinking. I will gather the stones and the materials."

Anya looked around the room, yearning to touch the fine needlework and linen that were hung with care about the room. Her mother taught her needlework, but her stitches were never as fine as this and her mother's were even better than her Aunt's. If Aunt Airmed or her mother were willing to sell even a small piece of embroidery, surely a city doctor could come and bring the color back into her mother's cheeks and the strength back into her heart.

Airmed set a china plate down in front of Anya. A buttery pastry filled with cinnamon-laced squash and an acorn filling lay upon it, steam rising in a swirl. The scent cut through Anya's fear and frustration. "Eat," Airmed called from across the room.

Anya stared at her. "How is it warm? Your oven is not lit."

Turning from the cupboard, Airmed said "I had it laid in front of the fire. There is no magic there, just basic common sense."

Anya bit into the pastry and the sweet and savory mixture of pumpkin, cinnamon and salt hit her tongue. Anya shook her head. How could her aunt possibly get these spices when she never left the island? Flakes of golden dough dropped into her lap, and she lifted the embroidered linen napkin to pick them up. Staring at the edge of the napkin, Anya was transfixed by the spirals and triskeles stitched in golden thread. The wind outside blew the sweet, cool scent of falling leaves in the open window and Anya heard the pulsating screech of the hawk owl.

Airmed turned to the window, eyes wide with alarm. A single golden leaf floated in the window and landed at her feet. Both women stared at it for a moment until Airmed picked it up and marched it over to the hearth where she tossed it in the flames. "No," she muttered. "There is a still a chance." She returned to the kitchen and brought several bowls to the table where Anya sat.

"Listen carefully, Eilidh," Airmed gave her niece a sharp look. "This is how we will save your mother."

CHAPTER FOUR

Airmed pointed to an iron bowl covered in swirls and spirals. "Eilidh," she said firmly. "Your mother needs strength in her blood. Has she been eating the greens and the fish I sent last time?"

"My father purchases beef for her and lamb. He says they are very dear."

Airmed rolled her eyes. "Your mother's life should be more dear to him than any pound of flesh. Perhaps if he had not insisted on a son after the last time..." Airmed's hand clenched around the jar she was holding.

A tear finally escaped and drifted down Anya's cheek. She looked at her folded hands in her lap. "A daughter is not enough."

"You are enough." Airmed stared at Anya until the girl looked up and met her eyes. "Do you hear me, Eilidh?" Anya's tears fell freely now. "You are strong and you are enough. Enough to change your life and change the lives of those around you. If you want to." She carefully brushed some of the wet from Anya's cheeks and walked over to the fire. She shook the tears into the flames and marched back to the table.

"Stop this now," Airmed said. "Stop your tears. They will help no one and achieve no gain. Now, watch carefully what I show you."

Airmed pointed to a jar of ground red powder. "This is jasper stone. I have ground it in this bowl you see here with an iron pestle. Jasper - she is the healer, both of spirit and of body. When you get home, you will brew your mother some tea with these herbs." Airmed set a bundle of dried herbs in front of Anya. "Yarrow, coriander, and motherwort." Airmed passed a length of embroidered linen. "Wrap the herbs in this cloth and listen. Build a fire in the hearth. When the flames are high, stir clockwise in the flames and say these words: Strength of the Body. Strength of the Mind. Strength of the Spirit."

Anya stared. She had often heard her mother whisper into the flames, but never in front of her father, and she had not told Anya yet what she was saying.

"Eilidh." Airmed's voice cut through Anya's thoughts. "Pay attention. Say those words exactly as you stir the flames." Airmed took a second jar out of the pocket of her apron. "This is agate, granite, and basalt. The agate will protect her spirit, the granite will hold her to the earth, and the basalt will bring the fire back into her veins. When your fire is lit and you have spoken the words, sprinkle this into the fire three times. Preserve some though, you may need to use it." Airmed passed the jar across the table. Anya stared at the shimmering dust within.

"When you have done that," Airmed continued, "Grind the herbs and make a tea. Then, you will heat the brewed tea over the flames in this iron bowl. Sprinkle one spoonful of ground jasper into the tea and stir, clockwise, do you understand? Stir until the jasper powder is dissolved. As you stir, whisper again, Strength of body, strength of mind, strength of spirit."

Anya leaned forward. "Mariloup will be watching the whole time, she won't let me do all of that, much less feed Mama the tea."

"Mariloup has been watching your father since we were in the schoolhouse. She'll be watching and she will be there, but you are stronger than her. Do you want your mother to have a chance or not?"

Anya's hazel eyes turned to ice. "I would do anything for her."

Airmed grasped the girl's hands in her own. "You are her only chance, Eilidh. You are her life."

CHAPTER FIVE

It had been eight days. Anya had done everything Airmed had instructed, every evening after supper. Her mother's eyes were so sunken. Color came to her mother's face for a time after she drank the tea, but her hands began to take on a yellowed hue. Mariloup was a constant presence, finding an excuse to come over each day when her father returned from fishing, always with fresh baked bread and a cloying scent applied to her neck. The woman would position herself by Liora's bedside, carefully arranging herself so that her dark hair gleamed in the firelight.

For eight evenings, Anya met Cillian as the twilight settled over the cliffsides. She said she was going to gather herbs and her father was so tired from his days at sea that he didn't question her.

Tonight, Anya checked to make sure her mother was asleep and Mariloup had truly left before she pulled her wrap around her shoulders. She closed the wooden door behind her. The wind felt dark and blue.

Anya walked the path up to the cliffside where Cillian would be waiting. His hands would not smell of fish like her father's did. He had learned to play the small Irish harp from an early age, he had a natural gift. He played for town ceremonies, for the church on Sundays, and lately, for her alone every moonrise on the cliffside. She knew if she was seen meeting him after sunset, they would have to marry.

Anya heard the strings of the harp as she walked up the path, the grasses brushing against her woolen skirt. He heard her footsteps and looked at her the way he did - that long look from under the shock of brown curls and his knit cap. As she ascended the cliffside, he wove the music higher. He kept his eyes locked on hers as she walked and her breath caught. It seemed that the grasses swayed and the wind swirled with the notes he played, until she seemed to be moving with the music of the whole earth.

His music. As she sat down on the flat rock near to him, the sea air blew the curls loose from her chignon. Leisurely, he finished his tune and walked over to her. His hands were calloused from stroking the strings and she leaned into the touch of his fingers as he held her face close for a kiss. Anya felt like she couldn't breathe. He tasted of salt air and clean skin. She felt the scruff of his beard on her cheek. His hands passed slowly along her neck and down her back until he was holding her tightly. As he pulled her toward the ground, she pushed gently against his chest. Leaning away, he looked into her eyes, puzzled. "What's wrong?"

"My mother." Anya gently released herself from his grasp and pulled her wrap back around her shoulders.

"You're shivering." Cillian reached for her hand and squeezed it before tightening his own coat against the wind.

"It's not working," she said. Cillian shifted and settled down on the ground next to her so his back was to the cliffside. The sea wind whipped Anya's hair and it blew into her eyes.

"The doctor's medicines?" asked Cillian.

"The herbs and... powders that my aunt gave to me." Cillian raised his eyebrows. Anya removed her hand from his grasp and tucked it into her pocket. "She isn't what they call her, you know."

"I didn't call her anything," Cillian said.

"She brought the stones and the plants over from Scotland when she immigrated. With my mother."

"How could she possibly bring the stones that built that house on a boat?" he asked.

Anya shook her head. "I think they found them on the island."

"There are no stones like that around here." Cillian stood up and went to wrap up his harp. "I don't know what your family tells you, my love, but there has to be more to that story."

14

"It's not a story." Anya looked out at the sea spray as it crashed on the rocks below. "There are stones right there. This whole cliffside is rock."

"Yes, but the agates and granites and whatever else she has on the island – you can't find them here," Cillian said.

"Jasper," Anya whispered.

"Jasper." Cillian nodded as he fastened the last clasp on the harp's case. "They're very valuable. They could make a life very comfortable. No worrying about having to go out to the damnable sea to fish, to gather those lobster. The insects of the sea world. Did you know that?"

"Insects of the sea world?" The leaves blew off the tree limbs in eddies. A maple leaf, scarlet and veined with amber fell onto her skirts.

"I learned that at University. Yes, lobster are just giant sea insects. Can't you see it when you look at them? If your father would go to that Island and sell some of the stones, he wouldn't have to go out to the sea each day foraging and he could be comfortable, easy. Rest in his years. And we, if we could be together..." He walked over to Anya and set the harp under a tree before kneeling before her and kissing the tear off of her cheek. "What is it?" His voice was husky as he breathed into her neck.

"My mother is sick." Anya stood and tucked the little birch leaf into the pocket of her skirt. "I have to go back."

"Anya, wait." Cillian hurried down the path and stepped in front of her, grasping her arms. "I'm sorry." Tears filled his eyes. "I'm so sorry." He gathered her slight body in his arms and she leaned against his chest, unable to weep. She wondered again what it would be like when they were married. Why couldn't they marry now? He could protect her from all of this - she could make a home for him. With him. It would be filled with music and she would sing. They wouldn't have to be like normal people, he wouldn't go to the sea and come home smelling like fish; his socks and coat wet for days. He didn't make much of an income playing the harp, but they could leave - go to Montreal. Or she could work; selling embroidery or mending. Why had he not asked her? She had given herself to him, careful of the cycles of the moon, and he had spoken so many times of being together, surely now he would ask and this nightmare would be over. He gripped her more tightly and she felt his kisses in her hair.

She pulled away.

"I have to go home. The light is fading."

"Stay with me," Cillian took her face in his hands and placed a fluttering kiss on her lips. "For just a little while longer."

"I can't. Not tonight."

Cillian took a deep breath and lowered his hands. He stepped back, forced himself to smile. "I understand. Of course I understand. Can I walk you home?"

"Cillian, you know if anyone sees us, there would be hell to pay."

Cillian stepped toward her again "That's why you should stay. We don't have to - I could just hold you. Be here for you. We could watch the moon rise and you could go home after the family was asleep."

"It's a new moon. Even more reason for me to walk home quickly." Cillain sighed.

"You're right," he said, looking at the sky. "Your father wouldn't like to see me at the door," he said. "I know I'm not good enough for him. For you. That's what they all say. That we should never be married."

"Cillian..." That word. The word she had been longing for that would carry her away from this entire mess.

"Go ahead home, Anya." Anya stepped toward him but he put out a hand to stop her. He looked at her sadly. "It's alright." Cillian lifted his harp onto his shoulders and walked away from her towards the forest path.

Turning her back to the sea, Anya made her way down the path, into the moonless night.

CHAPTER SIX

Anya looked out of the window, standing on her tiptoes to see the wash of stars over the indigo sky. Her father had long since been in bed, but her mother seemed restless tonight. More talkative than she had been in weeks.

"The tea is boiling, darling." Anya turned to the sound of her mother's weak voice. "Get the kettle before it wakes your father." Anya hurried to the stove and moved the kettle off the flame. The pink teapot with its golden spout and handle was ready on the counter. "Hot the pot," her mother whispered. Anya smiled at the unnecessary reminder. She poured a bit of boiling water into the pot and swirled it clockwise. Next, she placed the herbs in and poured the water in. The heavy iron bowl sat on the trestle table. Anya placed it near the hearth and poured the tea into it to heat, sprinkling the fine jasper powder in. "Strength of the body, strength of the mind, strength of the spirit," Anya whispered as she stirred.

Liora watched her daughter and sighed. "I'll only need that last one tonight," she whispered.

"Did you say something, Mama?" Anya turned away from the flames.

"No, Anya." Liora beckoned her daughter close. "It was only the wind you heard."

Anya brought a cup of tea to her mother's bedside and adjusted her pillows so she could sit up a bit. Once her mother had sipped the tea, Anya settled on a stool beside her.

"I should have taught you all of this long ago," Liora said, weakly patting the bed linen. Anya took her mother's cold hand in her warm one. "But then, I hoped there would be a brace of daughters. You could have taught your sisters..."

Anya pushed away the feeling of dread in her belly, like a scrape, a peeling back of everything that was known. "I thought you wanted a son," she whispered to the floor. Liora shook her head slightly.

"What I wanted..." her voice faded as she closed her eyes. Anya's head snapped up. Liora's eyes fluttered open again. "You were what I wanted. Your father was what I wanted. I have had what I wanted. Not, perhaps, what the world wanted from me, but I received what I wanted from the world." Liora coughed weakly and Anya hurried to remove the teacup and adjust the linen blankets closer around her mother.

"Mama, you should rest," Anya said. "You were so happy today, please rest so you can save your strength for tomorrow and it can begin to build again."

Her mother closed her eyes and settled into the covers. Anya stood silently to wash the teacup.

"You must not resent Mariloup." Anya turned again. Her mother's eyes were still closed. "Your father and I... what we had was real."

"You have Father, Mama. What are you saying?" Anya sat down again, teacup in her shaking hand.

"Yes, I do have Joseph." Liora smiled, though her eyes were still closed. "The world goes on. Mariloup will need someone to care for her. Your father will."

"I can take care of father," said Anya. "I can. You've taught me."

Liora took a raggedly breath. "Airmed will teach you. Spend time with her. Go to the Island. Learn the forging..." Liora coughed again. "The pictures in the stones..."

"Mama, please calm yourself. I'll visit Aunt Airmed. I promise you. Every day. And I'll care for father, Mariloup won't need to."

Liora opened her eyes and gazed at her daughter. "You will care for the person you love. And he'll care for you." A flush rose in Anya's cheeks and she struggled to meet her mother's eyes. Liora took a breath for strength. "You've been lucky, my girl... the choice you want to make..." Liora clenched her eyes closed. "It's not him. Your strength - is not his. It does not match."

"Mama, I love him." A tear fell onto Anya's cheek.

"No." Liora gave a weak squeeze on her daughter's hand. Tears fell from Anya's eyes.

"I need a handkerchief. I'll be right back, Mama."

Anya gently set her mother's hand on the blankets and wiped her nose with the back of her hand.

Liora turned to the stars shining through the window. "You'll take it forward for us all," she whispered.

"Did you say something, Mama?" Anya turned quickly.

"No, darling. I'm just the wind."

CHAPTER SEVEN

The trees in the churchyard were barren. A few specks of dirt clung to Anya's black silk glove. Her mother's black silk glove. Every fiber in her being wanted to run back to the horrible mound of earth, to cry, to scream, to keen. She watched her father, paler than he had ever been, black circles surrounding his dry eyes. Her mother would have wanted her to go home, to tend to him, to make the meals and feed him. To tend to the hearth.

Mariloup had brought coffee in the morning and poured out a glass of whiskey. Anya had risen before the sun to make the meal that would keep them standing through the service, including coffee with a dash of warmed cream just as her father liked it, but Mariloup had poured the cup unceremoniously in the sink. "Your father needs stronger stuff. Not a brew made by a child." She had reached out to brush Anya's hair but Anya had jumped back. "You may have some too." Anya had been drinking coffee with her parents for years. She was no child. Cillian had taught her that.

Anya had taken her father's arm on the breath-destroying walk to the churchyard, forcing Mariloup to walk with the two other widows of the town. As they passed the women, Anya had heard Mariloup whisper "It was a lucky thing Liora passed before the ground was frozen." Anya had wanted to turn around and slap her.

She searched the churchyard for her Aunt Airmed, but of course she wouldn't come. She couldn't leave the island. The mist coming off the ocean stung her face. There was nothing to do but return home with her father.

CHAPTER EIGHT

Tears flew freely down her cheeks as the wind whipped her loose hair. She paddled fiercely, recklessly, hardly able to see ahead. The island loomed in the distance. She could stay with Aunt Airmed, surely. Airmed would give her shelter. For she couldn't be in that house with Mariloup for another minute.

The woman had pushed Anya out of the kitchen and had taken over. Mariloup greeted guests as a hostess and whispered loudly enough for Anya to hear. Liora had always been weak, she said. Weak of body, weak of spirit. A woman who couldn't bear children for her husband was better off in heaven.

Was not Anya the gift of her mother's womb? Was she not her mother's child? Did she not help and assist her father?

Mariloup had "fixed" all of the dishes Anya had made for the repast. The night before the funeral, Anya was too numb to sleep, so she stood in the kitchen making all the recipes her mother had shown her - roast chicken with delicate sage dressing. Biscuits and cream.

The season was far past for strawberries, but Anya saved some apples from the harvest and used some of Aunt Airmed's precious cinnamon to make a stew to go with the fresh shortcakes. Mariloup had tasted each dish when she brought the coffee in the morning. Her father was sitting pale-faced at the table, a dish of apples and a hot shortcake before him. Noticing that Joseph was in earshot, Mariloup turned her voice sickly sweet. "These are a lovely tribute to your mother, Anya. But, I do think a bit of improvement is needed. Don't fret, you'll learn as you grow into a woman."

Anya stared her down with flinty eyes. "I cooked them exactly as my mother taught me," she said. "My father enjoys them this way."

Joseph looked up and said absently, "The shortcakes. They were my favorite." Mariloup looked at Joseph's stricken face and set her lips in a thin line.

"Sweets will not give you strength, sir." She stepped to the table. "And apples in the morning?" Mariloup tutted and removed the fragrant, steaming dish. "Those will turn your belly. Allow me to make you something more suitable." Mariloup had bustled into the kitchen and began to cook bacon. "Nice roasted meat, that's what a man needs in the morning." The sunlight caught something pinned to Mariloup's dress. A brooch, a shining crystal stone surrounded by smaller stones swirling with color. Anya had seen those stones somewhere before. The metalwork was of mediocre quality.

"Where did you get that brooch?" Anya asked. Mariloup reached up and patted it, a flash of pride flying across her features.

"It was a gift," she said, concentrating on the pan of bacon.

"From your late husband?" Anya remembered these stones. Remembered her mother asking her father to take them to Aunt Airmed, to have Airmed weave them into a bracelet. He could not have possibly...

"From your father." Mariloup flipped the bacon. Now she looked hard into the younger woman's eyes. "As a thank you. For all the things I did to nurse your mother."

The rest of the day was a blur. Friends and townspeople came in and gave their sympathy. Spoke soft, honest words about her mother, spoke of her kindness, her skill at needlework, her generosity and her beautiful voice. Liora had always sung for church services, she had taught Anya all the songs brought over from Scotland, some in English and some in Gaelic. Anya sang them too.

The salt from the waves mixed with the salt of her tears as she rowed closer to the island. She didn't think she could ever sing them again.

CHAPTER NINE

Airmed stood on the clear hillside of the island, black dress whipping in the wind. Anya could see her figure as she rowed close to shore. She saw her aunt calling out and could somehow hear her voice as if it was next to her in the boat.

"What are you doing, girl? Row to the cove."

Anya scanned the treeline. The leaves swayed to the north. Anya used all of her strength to turn the canoe sharply. Once at the protected cove, the wind at her back, she yanked it onto the rocks.

"You're going to injure yourself." Airmed walked along the sand. Anya looked at her - how had she climbed down from the hillside so quickly? "Or worse, put a hole in your boat. These rocks are jagged." Anya wiped her nose fiercely with the sleeve of her mother's black silk dress.

"Where were you?" Anya asked. She turned to her aunt, veins pulsating with anger and grief. "Didn't you think I would want you there? Didn't you want to be there??"

"Come out of the wind, Eilidh. We'll talk inside." Anya looked desperately around the shoreline. There was no other choice. She'd simply have to follow Airmed and keep walking.

The stone house rose before them, glittering in the pale winter sunshine. After discarding her cloak and gloves, Anya walked quickly to the hearth and began warming her hands in the flames.

Airmed stepped next to her niece and passed a cup of tea.

"I don't want it." Anya's teeth clenched and she refused to look at her aunt.

"Drink it. There's more in this brew than tea."

Anya suddenly snatched the hand-painted cup out of Airmed's hand. "Ground jasper? Herbs? They didn't work with my mother and they certainly won't work for me."

For a brief moment, tears threatened Airmed's creased eyelids. The older woman straightened her shoulders and put a firm hand on Anya's arm.

"Drink the tea. Now. It will give you strength."

Without breaking the gaze of her aunt, Anya threw back the entire cup of tea. Her eyes bulged as the hot, fiery liquid burned her throat and the flame of the whiskey blazed through her fury. Anya began to cough and sputter, and Airmed took the teacup and refilled it.

"Sip the tea. Sit down and sip it. Some days the magic of the stones is not enough. On days like this, we need the water of life." Airmed took Anya's free hand

and led her to a chair. Once Anya sat, Airmed moved to the cupboard and pulled out a beautifully knitted blanket, the rosettes of pinks, greens and blues. "I know it was a horrible day to be of the Earth," Airmed said, spreading the blanket on Anya's lap. "But you need to contain this fire inside you. Use it." Anya touched the red and pink yarn. It was soft as new lambs wool. The question still burned her throat.

"Why didn't you come?"

Airmed shook her head sadly. "Your mother needed to be remembered as the woman she chose to be. The healer, the midwife, the kind soul who sang at the church on Sundays. Wife to your father. And the town... the people deserved the chance to remember her without my sullying the past."

The strong drink was flushing to Anya's head, making her bold. "But what did you do, Aunt Airmed? Surely it couldn't be bad enough to never set foot on the mainland?" Airmed shook her head again and walked toward the hearth, hands on her hips.

"It was nothing I did. It was what I refused to do. Who I refused to be." The firelight lit her sharp cheekbones. "And what I knew. The knowledge I carried. Your mother can... could..." A small sob escaped her lips and she coughed it back. "Your mother was allowed to have the knowledge of forgery, of stonework, of healing because she lived a life that society agreed with." Airmed turned to Anya. "She submitted to a man. Married your father."

29

"Had me..."

"Of course she had you, Eilidh, giving the World a daughter was a duty she dreamed of fulfilling." Airmed looked at Eilidh as if she had said the most foolish thing in the world. "But in submitting to your father, she had to hide some of what she really knew. Of course it was all well and good to make pretty jewels, but the symbols, the power forged into the metal, she couldn't talk about that. And the songs she sang... you know the words were in Gaelic?"

Now it was Anya's turn to furrow her brow. "She sang in English."

"Well of course she did - she sang for church. But the Gaelic words... they speak of a time before the world of men." Airmed held her hands before the fire. "Do you know them?"

"I know the tunes. She sings..." Anya swallowed hard. "She would sing sometimes over the fire or when she was in the forge. Not in English - I assume in Irish. I learned some of it."

Airmed looked at her niece. "If she had only taught you the Song of Life." The older woman brushed a tear from her own cheek. "Ah well." Airmed said almost to herself. "She had lost so many babies, I knew this was coming."

"My father." Anya moved the blanket from her lap and began to pace the room. Airmed's sharp eyes followed her movement like a deer. "I guess one child wasn't enough. I guess I wasn't enough. He had to have a son and he had to kill her to get one."

Airmed stood and held out her hand. "Stop." She gestured to the chair. "You have no idea where the truth lies in that story."

Anya flew around to face her aunt, her dark hair plastered to her wet cheeks.

"Yes I do! He wanted a son - he had to have a son and he was willing to let her die to get one!"

"Sit down Anya. Drink your tea." Anya stomped over to the chair and snatched the teacup from the handhewn table. Again, she took the entire contents in one gulp and felt the fire of the whiskey fly to her belly and then to her head. She stumbled and felt Airmed pulling her into the chair. "Don't be a fool, girl." Airmed produced an embroidered handkerchief and sat in the chair opposite. "Your father loved her. And, he loved you. He never wanted more children, after your mother lost your brother. Your mother wanted a brood of babies and he tried to stop her, to insist, but her beauty and her strength... Well. He is a man. And men will do what they do."

Anya's head was spinning. She felt bile rising in her throat and her stomach turned over. She squirmed to jump out of the chair quickly but before she could move, Airmed stood before her with the slop bucket. Anya leaned over it and retched. Airmed rubbed her back until she was finished. After she had taken care of the slop bucket, Airmed came over with a handful of fresh, green

31

leaves. "Mint. Chew on it. Slowly." Anya stared at the herbs. What could possibly still be growing this close to winter? "It will settle your stomach. Airmed reached over and tucked the blanket around her niece. "What have you eaten today?" Anya shook her head and she struggled to nibble on the mint leaf. "Nothing?" Airmed asked. "But surely there was food brought by the neighbors?"

"There was, and I made all of Mama's recipes, but I had to greet everyone and feed my father, and Mariloup _"

Airmed scoffed and brushed the idea away. "That pinched, desperate woman has had her eye out for your father since we were children. Don't let her worry you. Now. I will make you some toasted bread with a sprinkle of sugar to settle that stomach of yours." Airmed glanced wryly at the teacup. "I thought that may have been a bit strong for you, but I didn't realize you had nothing in your stomach."

Airmed poured Anya a glass of fresh water from the stream. She got to work toasting the fresh brown bread and soon Anya was settled with pillows, a second woven afghan, and refreshments. "Do you feel better?" Airmed asked.

"In body," Anya said quietly.

"Do you feel strong enough to tell me about the day?" Airmed asked. Anya sighed deeply. She looked at her aunt and saw trust there. Saw the older woman's own deep and abiding grief. She sat up straight and haltingly began to tell all that had occurred.

When she got to Mariloup, Airmed put up her hand. "You can't prevent that. It will happen. Mariloup's children are grown. She won't have any more. Your father needs someone to care for him and that person cannot be you. You must live your life."

Anya fingered the blanket in her lap and looked at the roaring fire in the hearth. It was cozy here, safe. And there was plenty of room.

"Eilidh." Her aunt's voice was full of sorrow. "No." Anya met her eyes, silently pleading with Airmed. "I'm sorry," Airmed said." "There is nothing that would make me happier, but..."

"I could help you, Aunt. I could go to the mainland and get whatever you needed."

"I don't need help."

Anya looked out of the window at the gale blowing the last of the leaves off the trees. "I do," she whispered.

Airmed was kneeling at her side. She placed a warm, dry hand on Anya's sleeve. "Help I can give, my dear." She reached up and lifted her niece's chin. "I can teach you. I can teach you the songs, the forge, the metal working and all the secrets of the stones. I can make sure you know the powers of the herbs."

"Why can't I stay?" Anya asked.

"Because I stayed. I stayed and I learned and I worked and I never tied myself to a man or gave children to the world. I had the audacity to believe that that would be enough. That my knowledge and assistance

33

and power would be enough. That the people would value that; embrace it. Instead, they abandoned me. Slurred me and slurred the knowledge I had earned and the gifts I could give. I thought I was protected here when truly I have been locked away."

"Oh Aunt." The sympathy melting in Anya's fiery eyes made Airmed's throat catch. She patted the younger woman's arm and stood up.

"I never wanted more. I never wanted the home and the man and the children. I had what I wanted. I earned it. Your mother... your mother thought she could do both. Have both. She married the man and had you and had wonderful standing in her community, but she had to hide the extent of what she could do."

"But she did make the jewelry and she did use the herbs to help people heal. Especially new mothers," Anya said.

"You said yourself that she would never sing the true Irish words to the songs. She would only sing in English. Is that right?" Airmed asked. Anya furrowed her brow. "And when she gave the herbs, did she tell the women which words to say? Even in English? Did she give anyone a Ceremony?" Airmed gave Anya a long look. "I thought not." Airmed scoffed quietly. "So you see, she was trapped as well."

"But I won't be, and I don't even know all the skills. What is a Ceremony?" Anya asked.

Airmed's eyes widened. "Your mother didn't tell you about the Ceremony?" She stood and paced the room. Finally, she went to the window. Looking outside, she asked, "Will your father miss you tonight?"

Anya looked at her. "He asked me to row to you. To tell you."

"Well, it's too dark to begin the journey back. You'll stay here tonight." Airmed nodded brusquely at the barren trees in the woods. "Your father will understand." She turned back to Anya.

"We'll talk about the rest in the morning."

CHAPTER TEN

The dawn light filtered in the window. Underneath the lace coverlet and piles of woven blankets, Anya's eyes fluttered open. She breathed in the earthy, ancient scent of the stone wall and the sharp, fresh scent of the fragrant lavender that rested in a jar at her bedside. She remembered where she was and a split second later, she remembered why she was there. Like the bile from the night before, a sob came fiercely and unexpectedly from her throat.

Airmed opened the bedroom door. "Let your tears flow. Until the sun is above the horizon. It is right and it is natural. When you have watered the Earth, come into the kitchen. We will have tea."

After Anya had exhausted all of her tears, she wiped her face and nose with the handkerchief that Airmed had placed at the bedside, and sipped from the mug of fresh water she must have left. Even through her haze of grief, Anya wondered at the incredible finery of the handkerchief's embroidery. Only the truly wealthy owned things like this. Just selling this piece would bring in more than her father made in a fortnight. She would ask her aunt. Ask her to tell her the secrets. Fresh linen was laid by her bed and a dress of darkest indigo hung on the handle of the cupboard. Pinned to it was a note:

"Your mother has returned to the place from whence we all come. She is part of the sky now; the air we breathe, the clouds that hold the water that gives life to the fields, and the fire in the starlight. Wear this dress of the night sky in her honor."

Anya wiped tears away. She poured water from the cream pitcher on the table into the accompanying basin and splashed her face and neck. It was scented with dried orange and peppermint. She used one towel to pat her face dry and picked up the other. Dipping it in the fragrant water, she quickly washed herself. She pulled the gown over her head and fastened the buttons. The deep blue made her skin glow and brought out the subtle auburn streaks in her dark brown hair. Anya loosened her hair from the nighttime braid, brushed it out and re-pinned it into a chignon atop her head.

When she emerged into the kitchen, Airmed was waiting with an apron and a cloak. She handed Anya the cloak first. "Go out and take care of your needs and bring back the last of the lemon balm from the garden. This morning we will learn a bit of herbology. Once we've prepared breakfast and made some foodstuff for you to bring home, I will show you the forge. You must learn to work with the stones and create the jewelry." She glanced out of the window, checking the placement of the sun in the sky. "And you must start for home before the evening, so go quickly."

Anya looked around the warm room, every seat covered in quilts, blankets. Dried, fragrant herbs hung on twine from every window frame. The stones sparkled in the firelight. "Aunt, could I not stay here?" she asked. Airmed shook her head.

"You must return to your father's house. There is much more for you than what is on this island." Airmed set the kettle atop the flames on the stove. "But you can return each week, for three days. You may stay the night. If you are willing to learn quickly and pay attention, I can teach you the skills of our family before the winter is over." Anya's eyes lit up. She walked hesitantly to her aunt and embraced her.

"Thank you," Anya whispered. "And thank you for the dress."

Airmed stepped back and placed both hands on the younger woman's pale cheeks.

"Always."

CHAPTER ELEVEN

"Careful." Cillian laughed lightly as Anya stumbled on the cliffside. Gently, he withdrew his hand from hers. "I still have to play on Sunday. Take my arm instead." Anya turned toward the sound of the sea to hide the color rising in her face. He elbowed her gently. She turned to him.

"You know that they asked me to sing," she said. "The songs my mother sang."

Cillian cocked his head. "The pastor talked to you?" he asked.

"Well, he talked to my father." Anya said.

"And what did your father say?" Cillian asked, putting his hands behind his back.

"He said it would be unseemly. Too soon. I don't know..." Anya swallowed hard. "I could have done it."

Cillian breathed a sigh and Anya looked sharply at him. Was it relief she saw in his eyes? He had always told her that her voice was good, decent, when they played on the cliffside together. "Well, it would be very emotional for you," Cillian said. "And you know, you're not trained."

"Like you?" Anya stopped walking.

"Anya, it's no use denying what is true. I had four years of training at the Conservatory. They train musicians not only in technique and in repertoire, but in the skills to subvert your personal feelings into the music. To serve the music, if you will. It's very difficult not to be overcome by emotion when you perform beautiful music. And if you allow yourself to be overcome by the sadness, by the aching, it's a selfish act."

"Selfish." Anya repeated the word. She lifted her heavy skirts and began to walk up the hill. Cillian shook his head and followed.

"You're doing it now," he said.

"What?" Anya asked.

"You're allowing yourself to be overcome by your feelings. We can't even have a conversation without you stomping away," Cillian reached out for her arm.

"I was not stomping. The snow is getting deep."

"If you say so," Cillain said. "Anya, what I was saying is that if you give into your own sadness, your own aching, the love in your own heart, you deny that to the music. And then you deny it to the audience. The people who came to hear you play. Who came to be moved in a way no other force on Earth could move them. By the music."

"I have talent. And skill." Anya snatched her elbow out of his hand.

"I'm not denying that. Of course you do. Your talent is almost natural. But you don't have the training I have. And that's as it should be. So let me do this for you. Let me play on Sunday and allow you to feel all the things you are feeling," he said. "Uninhibited."

Anya rubbed her hands together against the cold.

"Where are your gloves?" Cillian asked, laughing.

"I left them at the stone house. On the Island," Anya said.

"How did you possibly row across the bay in this weather without gloves?"

Anya raised one eyebrow at him. "I have years of training."

Cillian smiled ruefully. "Speaking of training, what is your aunt teaching you? Are you learning that fine embroidery?"

"Some," Anya said. "I'm learning healing techniques, and how to work the forge. She's teaching me - well, she's teaching me the songs." Cillian nodded. "And the mysteries of the stones."

At this, Cillian rolled his eyes. "You should learn the value of the stones."

"I am. Each stone has spiritual significance, like granite for example - "

"No, not some made-up legend." Cillian took her cold hands in his gloved ones. "I mean the monetary value. Anya, don't you see? The jewelry your mother made, that your aunt is teaching you to make, has real value. The embroidery, what little I've seen of it, is of the quality carried by the wives of the richest benefactors in Montreal. The value of those could be life changing."

"For me?" Anya asked. "People in town don't have the money to buy real jewels, so my mother always sold them for what people could pay."

"For us." Cillain drew her into a hug. "You are learning skills that could far surpass what any of us could make in a year. Imagine what that could mean. We could go to Montreal; I could play for real concert halls, for cathedrals."

"You would marry me?" Anya asked

"We would go to Montreal, together!" Cillian said. "Look at this," he lifted the sleeve of her cloak, which she had embroidered under the instruction of Airmed. When she had finished the sleeve, Airmed had admitted that her needlework surpassed even her own.

"Did your aunt do this?" Cillian asked.

"I did that," Anya said, running her finger along the fine stitches. Cillian beamed at her and kissed her fully on the lips.

"You. You are incredible. Think of what a life we could live. You could make a living selling these and I could play music, and Anya..." He put one beautiful hand on her cold cheek. "We could leave this village. We wouldn't have to live an ordinary life."

Anya reached up and put her hand on top of his. He shuddered at her touch. "Your hands are freezing," he said. "If your hands made this, they deserve to be warm." Cillian took off his own gloves and placed them on

Anya's hands. "Come," he said. "The grove is sheltered, and I brought a bit of firewood."

"It's freezing," Anya protested.

Cillian kissed her again. "We'll find a way to stay warm."

CHAPTER TWELVE

Anya took the silver out of the forge and bent over it with her tools.

"Careful," Airmed whispered. She reached out toward Anya, but then stepped away as she saw the young woman work. "By the Spirit, those spirals are perfectly formed."

Anya heard nothing her aunt had said. She gracefully brushed the tip of her pick over the steaming, soft metal. Once she was satisfied with her design, she placed the metal in the white snow to cool. She added the glue and placed the jasper stone in its holder. Pressing it with her fingers, she said the words Airmed had taught her in a clear, low voice.

"May the spirals etched here free my mind from worldly concerns. May my thoughts fly freely as the clouds, and enter the highest reaches of heaven. I ask this by the Air. May the flames in which this metal was forged burn eternally in my heart. I ask this by the Fire. May the water that cools and sets the art help me flow to new pathways. I ask this by the Water. And may this stone serve as a map to guide my life where the Spirit would have me go. I ask this by the Earth. I bless this jewel by all the elements and by the Spirit, who lives and works in me."

"Amen," said Airmed.

A gust of wind blew through the air and brought Anya out of her trance. "Did I do alright?" She asked out of politeness, for the surge of power and love flowing through her veins gave her more answer than her aunt ever could. For her part, Airmed lifted the jewel. "This is more exquisite than any piece I've ever made, or any piece your mother made. It's more beautiful even than the pieces your grandmother made." Airmed looked at Anya. "Eilidh, how did you do this?"

Anya merely shrugged.

"Why do you call me Eilidh?" she asked instead.

"It is your given name," Airmed said. She handed the jewel to Anya. Taking the chain off her own neck, she handed that over as well. "Here. Until you forge something of your own." Anya took the still warm pendant and slipped it onto the silver chain. Airmed stepped behind her and made to fasten it to her neck. "Lift your hair," she said, and Anya lifted her loose dark tresses. Once the stone was settled at the valley of Anya's chest, Airmed moved to stand by her. "Eilidh," she said. "Your mother gave you this name when you were born. Here, on the Island. Your father agreed."

"My father was here?" Anya

"Of course," Airmed said.

Anya couldn't believe her father would agree to such a name. He didn't believe in using the old Gaelic. "Live in the world in which you find yourself." he always said. When Liora would sing too clearly in the old Gaelic, he would say simply, "We're not in Scotland." Her mother would smile her apology under her lashes and continue the song in English.

"Look up at the sky," Airmed said. "The sun shines even in the coldest of winter days. The light is still there. And that's what your name means. Sun ray. Shining light." She took the girl's hands in her own. "And that is what we expect you to be: a shining light to the world. Even in darkness." Airmed glanced at the roiling sea just past the woodland. "Especially in darkness."

The women walked back to the stone cottage after closing up the forge. Airmed began to pack her basket of herbs and baked goods. This time, she put a few small clay pots of potted lavender and mint in the basket and wrapped them carefully in burlap.

"You need to learn to tend to these at home," Airmed said. "And really, we should practice the Ceremony. Your words are so beautiful and you speak them so well, I'm curious..." She stopped and gave a quick glance to Anya. "Well. We can only do what we can in the time we have."

"Tell me again, Aunt," Anya asked. "Who is allowed to have a Ceremony?"

"People who are willing," Airmed said. "People who have the wisdom. The creativity. The love. At the very least, people who are willing to work to attain it."

Anya pulled the basket away and touched her hand to her aunt's. "You said that I had my Ceremony when I was a baby. How could you possibly know if I possessed those traits or if I would be willing to attain them?"

"You were the daughter of your mother. A daughter of the family. It was without question."

"But who else?"

Airmed wiped her hands brusquely on her apron. "Who else could have the Ceremony? People who wished to learn. Who could commit time to learning. And husbands, friends of the daughters of the family. Of course they must have the Ceremony, if for no other reason than to see if the stones are compatible."

"What about people who have other gifts? Brilliant gifts?"

Airmed laughed at this. "Who in that village could possibly have other brilliant gifts?"

"There is a man. A musician." Airmed was quick as a fox to hide her reaction to her niece's words.

"Music is one of the gifts of the Spirit," she said levelly. "Tell me more about this man. Is he courting you?"

A blush rose into Anya's cheeks, and she lifted her head proudly. "Yes. He is."

"How often do you see him?"

47

"Several evenings a week. We walk up to the cliffside."

"Evenings."

"I'm home by moonrise," Anya said quickly.

"Of course you are, Eilidh. I accuse you of nothing. So, the village knows."

"Actually, Cillian says it's better if the village doesn't know." Airmed could not repress a grunt. Anya threw her shoulders back. "He says that there is nothing that love cannot conquer. That that village people are ordinary and that they would not understand..."

Airmed put her hand up. "There are many things in life that love will not conquer." Her voice was low and deep. The older woman closed her eyes and took a shuddering breath. When she opened her eyes, she smiled at Anya. "Bring... Cillian - Is that his name?" Anya nodded. "Bring him with you next time."

Anya beamed. "Thank you, Aunt!" She leapt forward for an embrace. Airmed squeezed her hard and then gently pushed her back, holding her by the shoulders. Anya felt her aunt's sharp eyes scan her body, stopping briefly at her stomach. She met her aunt's eyes. She could find no question there.

Airmed went to a separate bureau by the drawer. "Take these." She handed Anya a packet of worn, soft linen, unembroidered. Anya blushed. "Your mother would have provided you with fresh ones. Allow me to do it in her stead." Anya took them with lowered eyes. "Oh come, Eilidh, we are both women here. There is no need for shame about the monthly courses. You must simply be clean and have honor for your body and the passage that brings all life to this world."

"Oh Aunt," Anya tucked the linens in the inner pocket of her cloak.

"Eilidh, I will not have that silliness here. Only truth. When are your courses due next?" Airmed asked.

"At the new moon," Anya muttered. Airmed nodded.

"It has just begun to wane," she said to herself with a measure of relief. Airmed reached back into the cupboard and pulled out several packets of dried herbs. "I want you to brew this tea every evening. Drink it. At least two cups."

"What will it do?" Anya asked.

"It will keep you protected through this winter," Airmed said, slamming the cupboard door shut. "And if Mariloup wants some, by all means pour her a cup." Anya rolled her eyes. Airmed looked at the sun. It was beginning to set although it was barely past midday. "Brew a separate pot for your father. He will not care for the taste of this. Too earthy." She tucked the packets deep in the basket. "Now you must begin your journey back to the mainland. I shall see you in three days. Bring the man Cillian and we shall see if he is ready for the Ceremony." Airmed wrapped her niece in a quick, tight embrace. "Be well and strong, Eilidh."

Anya nodded and stepped toward the doorway, but as her foot crossed the threshold, Airmed grabbed her arm and turned her around.

"And be careful."

CHAPTER THIRTEEN

Cillian wrapped his arms more tightly around his harp as Anya paddled the canoe across the waves. "I'm sorry," he said, teeth clenched. "Please try to stop splashing water onto the instrument." She looked at him.

"The wind is carrying water through the air, Cillian," she said. "I can't control the wind."

Cillian glared at her for a moment and turned to face the island. "How much longer will it take until we arrive?" he asked.

"A quarter of an hour if the wind stays at our back." Anya took the woolen blanket from her lap and passed it to Cillian. "Wrap the harp in this as well."

"It's wet." Cillian snapped as he picked up the blanket.

Anya stopped paddling for a moment and stared at him. "Put the dry side against the instrument. It's wool; it won't soak through."

Anya shivered as she lifted the paddle and continued to row. The wind blew them toward the cove soon enough and Anya disembarked to pull the canoe onto the shoreline. Cillian hopped lightly onto the snowy shore and looked around.

"Beautiful," he said appreciatively. "These trees… it looks like this forest has been untouched. The timber here alone…" He gave a long low whistle.

"The house is this way," Anya said. "Come along."

Airmed was not standing at the threshold to meet them as usual. Anya opened the door and called out. There was no answer, but a fire burned brightly in the hearth. She held the door open for Cillian. "Go in," she said. "Warm yourself by the fire." Cillian stepped inside, shaking snow onto the stone foyer. His eyes raked across the carved stone of the house, the plentiful, precious herbs drying in every windowsill, the fine china in the cabinet, and most of all the intricately embroidered and woven cloth draped on every surface. He smiled at Anya. "I'm starving," he said. Anya smiled at him, and he looked at her more closely. The harsh wind had brought a beautiful color to her cheeks and her eyes sparkled in the firelight. He stepped toward her and snatched her in a sudden embrace, kissing her deeply. "I've missed you," he whispered into her neck, inhaling her sweet scent. "It has been too long since we were properly together. If your aunt is away, perhaps we could…"

"Good morning, Eilidh." A strong, low voice sounded from the doorway. Cillian looked up and met sharp blue eyes. He blushed but only for a moment. He peeled himself away from Anya and strode toward Airmed, his boots leaving water prints on the floor.

"Ah, the famous Lady of the Island," he said, hands on his hips. "Thank you for inviting me to your beautiful home." Gesturing widely, he said, "The beauty of this place knows no bounds. It's incredible that you receive so few visitors."

Airmed regarded him coolly. "I prefer it that way." She handed him the carved box in her arms. "Now if you would not mind carrying this to the table." Stepping over the melting snow on the floor, she walked toward the stove. Anya followed nervously. Airmed said nothing as she handed her the kettle to fill, and Anya snuck a quick peek at her aunt's face. It was expressionless. Airmed did not speak nor meet Anya's eyes until the tea was brewing and the pastries had been placed on a warm serving platter. "Serve the refreshments, Eilidh."

Cillian looked up from unwrapping his harp. "Is someone joining us?"

"What do you mean, sir?" Airmed swished her skirts under her and settled herself at the table.

"Eilidh is my given name," Anya said. "Father thought it best to Anglicize it from the Gaelic version."

"Well, that's not quite the whole story, but there it is," said Airmed, pouring the tea. "Cream or sugar?" She asked Cillian.

"Oh both. Two lumps, if you can spare them. I like the sweet." He winked at Anya. Airmed poured the cream and dropped in two lumps, stirring counter-clockwise before handing the cup to Cillian. "Please," she said in a neutral voice. She poured tea for Anya and herself before saying, "I assume you are the great Harpist of the Mainland. Cillian."

Cillian held her gaze. "It's true I play the harp. I was schooled at Lanuaria Conservatory. Excuse the lack of humility, but I did graduate top of my class."

Airmed smiled at him and nodded.

"It is my dream to return to Montreal," Cillian said, sipping his tea. "Anya has said she believes that I could find success there. She wants to go as well." Cillian reached across the table and squeezed her hand. Anya felt the buttery pastry stick in her throat.

Airmed looked at the pair of them for a long moment. Finally, she said, "Marriage is a long business. It should only be taken on by those who are strong."

Cillian's smile faded from his eyes, but he forced his lips to remain upturned. "Adventure," he said, slapping the table lightly. "Adventure is what we are after, and adventures can only be undertaken by the strongest of them all."

"Well." Airmed nodded. "A successful adventure will require a roadmap. It should be bolstered by a community, and knowledge, and love."

"We have love," Cillian said, laughing. "We have love in spades." Anya's heart fell into her stomach. Cillian had never mentioned the word love before. She wished her aunt would pour a dram of whiskey in her tea.

"Then we must be sure you attain the other two." Airmed stood. "Cillian, I wonder if you would be so good as to play us a tune. It has been many seasons since I was blessed by the gifts of a true harpist."

Cillian gave a small bow. "Do you mind if I move my chair by the hearth?" Airmed smiled and gestured that he was welcome. The light from the flames made his dark curls glow. Music began to ebb and flow into the room. Anya closed her eyes and listened. She was always entranced by his playing, and tonight she was doubly overcome by the warmth of the room and sweet smell of the herbs. She allowed herself to lean back into the comfort of the linen blanket on the chair. Both Airmed and Cillian watched her as she relaxed her features and a smile spread across her face.

In a whisper, Cillian said, "Now for a song you have not heard yet, Anya." He began to play an otherworldly tune, full of aching, spinning, exhilarating rising, and depths beyond dreams. Anya fell deeper into her trance. She felt as if she could see the music float through the air, weaving around them all, binding wrists, sweetly brushing against their throats…

"Oh!" Airmed cried out hoarsely. "S… stop." She put out a shaking hand. "Stop. Please."

A discordant sound jolted Anya from her trance.

"Did you not like it?" Cillian looked surprised and not a little offended. Airmed rubbed her temples and looked at Cillian, face pale.

"Where did you learn that tune?" she breathed.

"At University," Cillian said, rubbing his hands together to keep them warm.

"They taught you the music from the Good Neighbors?"

"This is just an old Irish tune. I learned it at University; well, I did spend time in the archives. I wanted to learn something new; you see. Something no one else was skilled enough to learn." Looking to each of the women and receiving no praise, Cillian shook his head. "It was written on parchment," he said. "I wasn't allowed to choose it for the final performance, but as soon as I played it, I never forgot it. It stayed in my fingers."

"Of course it did," Airmed said. She looked to her niece. Anya's eyes were still cloudy as she gazed into the flames. "Eilidh," Airmed said sharply. Anya blinked and tried to focus on her aunt's face. "Has he played this for you before?"

"I have never heard such beautiful music in my life," Anya said, finally focusing her eyes on Airmed. Cillian looked at Anya, a smile spreading across his face. Airmed gave a shuddering breath.

"Well." Airmed rose from her seat. "Regardless of what I may think of you as a man, Cillian, it is clear that you have the strength enough to become part of Uisdeen Fireen. And talent to spare."

"What is Uisdeen Fireen?"

"Uisdeen Fireen is our Society. It goes back beyond memory. We take vows of wisdom, creativity, and love. We never stop working to attain them, and we spend our lives serving others with those gifts."

"What would I have to give? Is there a payment, because as you must know, even isolated on the Island as you are, ma'am, a humble musician such as myself does not have much to offer in terms of coin."

"You would give your commitment to attaining and using the Gifts. You would give your word that your life would be dedicated to study and service. If you agree, we can perform the Ceremony."

Cillian balked. "What Ceremony?"

Finally, Anya spoke. "The Ceremony a series of prayers. And the choosing of your stone." Cillian looked hard at her. "You would commit to yourself only. And the Spirit. Once your stone has chosen you, I will forge it into a jewel to wear." He began to smile. Wrapping up his harp, he asked, "Do you join with me, Anya?"

"I had my Ceremony as an infant. I will perform your Ceremony. You would be my first."

A soft laugh escaped Cillian's lips. Airmed threw him a sharp look before amending her features.

"And at the end of the Ceremony, I earn one of the pieces of stone jewelry?" he asked. "Like the beautiful jewel that you wear, Anya?"

"You are given your stone, yes." Airmed said.

"Well," said Cillian, rising from his stool. "Let us begin."

CHAPTER FOURTEEN

Anya raised the mantle over her shoulders and settled it on the crown of her head. The silk flowed down her back and shone in the firelight. On a second cloth, she laid several polished stones.

"Cillian Hughes," she said in a clear voice. "Breathe in the good air of this place and find the Fire that lies within you. Let your hand guide you to your Spirit Stone."

Cillian's eyes raked over the selection. His hand quickly passed over a stone that was dark as night and dotted with flecks like the stars in the sky. A perfectly round stone layered with milky pearl, lavender and coral made him pause, but its matte veneer caused him to continue. Next was a solid stone, maroon and pink in color, speckled with gray, purple and black. "That's just granite," Cillian muttered to himself.

Airmed sucked in her breath sharply.

Cillian lifted a cream-colored stone, streaked with indigo. Not finding what he wanted, he set it down.

A green stone was next, striped with brown and purple streaks, like pathways. Cillian looked up at Anya and smiled. "This looks like the stone you wear," he said.

"Jasper." Anya answered.

Cillian turned to Airmed. "I thought perhaps uncut emerald. Or jade?"

"Jade does not come from our homeland," said Airmed. "Nor, in fact, does Emerald." Cillian shrugged, and wrinkled his brow. There were two stones left. The first was perfectly circular and smooth, almost as white as the snow. The etching inside looked like mountains, like pink sky. Cillian's eyes went wide.

"Diamond," he breathed.

"Quartz." Airmed said calmly.

Cillian put a hand to his brow and rubbed his eyes. He had been staring at that stone since Anya had set them out. A diamond this size would have been unheard of, and could finance years, maybe decades in Montreal. He would have never believed that such a jewel existed, but after seeing the level of craftsmanship at the stone house, and the carving of the jewel stones themselves, he let himself think it was possible. He had even waited until nearly the end, pretended that this stone was not the first one that had caught his eye.

"You must choose a stone." Airmed's voice cut through his thoughts. Cillian tried not to glare at her as he met her eye. She held his gaze steadily. He offered a small smile.

"Of course." The final stone was a misshapen lump, but it seemed to catch all the fire from the hearth and let the light sparkle back out through its surface.

Cillian could hardly believe that alongside what he had thought was a diamond, Anya and her aunt had set out such a sizeable nugget of gold. This gold had more luster than he had ever seen. It was a warmer yellow, like the leaves in fall, and each sharp edge was like a silver mirror reflecting all the light in the room. Cillian had thought gold was a metal, not a stone, but looking at this, perhaps gold began as a stone. He shook his head. This was not knowledge he needed, he thought. He had studied musical arts, not scientific ones. In any case, this chunk of gold may not finance decades in Montreal, but it would certainly buy him fare and a place to live when he arrived.

Cillian made a show of looking again at a few of the other stones, palming each one and closing his eyes as if in prayer. He memorized where the gold piece lay and with his eyes still closed, waved his hand across the table until he landed just above it. "This..." he intoned softly. "This feels right." Reaching down, he lifted the stone and opened his eyes. "My Stone," he said, meeting Anya's gaze.

"Your Spirit Stone," corrected Airmed. She stepped forward and put a hand on Anya's back. "Finish the blessings, Eilidh."

Anya recited the final blessings of Ceremony, dedicating the stone and Cillian to the four elements and to the Spirit. When she had finished and extinguished the candle, Cillain grinned. "Thank you very much. Shall I play my harp again?"

The thought of hearing the songs of the Good Neighbors once more brought sharp pain to Airmed's temple. "No," she said. "Thank you. We have done much today and I'm sure you are tired. I know I am. Anya must return to her father's house before twilight. Now, Cillian, if you would give me your stone- "

"Give it to you?" he asked, drawing his clenched hand to his chest. "I'm sorry, I thought it was mine. To keep."

"It will be," said Anya. "After we set it into a bracelet. Or pendant if you'd like."

Cillian knew that although the silver the women used to make jewelry was in itself valuable, he was sure they would have to shave off a bit of the golden stone to set it properly. He could not risk losing any of the value now that he had it.

"Anya," he said. "I… It means so much that you've blessed me with this stone. Airmed, it's an honor just to be allowed on this isolated Island." He reached across the table and squeezed Anya's hand. With a tight grip, he stroked the top of her hand with his thumb. "Playing that music for you – it feels like I left a part of myself here." Still holding Anya's hand, he looked at Airmed. "Please," he asked. "Let me take the stone today. In payment for the part of myself I left here when I played for you."

"It will remind you of the day when you wear it on a pendant forged from our hearth," said Airmed, raising one eyebrow. "But, yes, as you say. It is yours to do with as you wish. If you'd like to keep it…"

"I would," Cillian said firmly to Airmed. Turning back to Anya, he said, "Would it be too much to ask to wrap it in one of those cloths?"

Anya looked to Airmed, and the elder woman nodded her approval. Anya went to the bureau and retrieved a napkin and a handkerchief. Cillian pointed to the napkin. Anya spread the larger piece of linen out on the table and gestured for Cillian to set the stone he held onto the cloth. Carefully, he set it down and leaned in as Anya wrapped it. Her swift fingers folded the edges and began to wrap the rock and as she did, golden dust flaked onto the napkin.

"Careful, dammit!" Cillian hissed. His face was contorted in a way Anya had not seen before. "Please. It's valuable."

"It is valuable for its powers of protection and shielding, you mean," Airmed said.

Cillian thought of the heavy stone's ability to protect him and shield him – from hunger, from want, from spending a life in manual labor when his talents allowed him so much more. He grabbed the wrapped bundle from the table. "That's exactly what I mean," he said.

Airmed walked to Anya and gently removed the mantle from her hair. "You must go, Eilidh." She glanced at Cillian. "Be sure you go straight to your father's house. I have a premonition he will need you this evening. I shall see you back here when the moon is new."

Anya wrinkled her nose. "But that's only two days from now. Usually I come every Sunday. And it's dangerous to paddle across with so little light."

"The wind will guide you," Airmed said. "Goodnight."

CHAPTER FIFTEEN

The little boat glided onto the sandy shore as the sun disappeared behind the trees. Anya waited for Cillian to gather his harp and disembark before she dragged the canoe up into the wood. "Are you sure you cannot walk up to our cove with me?" Cillian asked, pulling her behind a tree. He kissed her hard, and wrapped his arms around her back, holding her close. Anya pulled her head away and tucked her face into his shoulder.

"I can't," she said. "I have to return to my father's house."

"Please." Cillian pushed his body against hers. "I need you."

Anya gently pushed him away. "It's been a very exhausting day, Cillian. Tomorrow?"

He sighed, leaning his head down and laying it on her chest before straightening up. He adjusted the harp slung on his back. "If you insist." Smiling at her, he turned and walked away.

As Anya walked up the path toward her house, she could see the lights blazing through the lace curtains. She quickened her step to the front gate.

"Oh, Anya!" cried Mr. Burke, the church warden. "You are so like your mother; I thought we had seen a ghost."

"Hello, sir," Anya said, furrowing her brow at the noise coming from the house.

"Your father said you were on the Island bringing supplies to your aunt, but we're so glad you're here to celebrate the news!"

"Celebrate?"

Joseph stepped over the threshold. When he saw his daughter, the relief that shone on his face washed away. He clenched his strong jaw and held out his hand. Anya took it and let her father help her up the slippery steps. "There's more beer inside, Burke," he said, nodding toward the doorway.

"Anya," Joseph said, closing the door behind him. "I… I didn't quite know how to tell you. After all, you've been gone so much, on the Island, or taking your walks in the evenings, it was difficult to find the time. I know this may be hard, but it had to be done. I'm going to marry Mariloup."

"What?" Anya tried to withdraw her hand, but her father held firm.

"It's for the best. I love... loved… your mother as much as…" Joseph swallowed and looked out at the darkening sky. "But she's gone. It's no use pretending otherwise. And she would want me to be cared for."

"I can care for you! She taught me everything!"

"You will care for your husband, and children of your own. That is the life you are meant to live. The life she wanted for you."

"Mariloup is…" Anya choked on her words, a tear sliding down her cheek.

"Mariloup needs someone to care for, like all women do. She cared for your mother, didn't she? And they were friends, as children. We all were." Joseph looked at the horizon and swallowed hard. He couldn't see the heartbreak that hid beneath the storm on his daughter's face. "Mariloup has a soft heart; you'll see. And you." Joseph reached out and chucked her on the chin. Anya realized that it was the first time she'd seen her father smile since her mother fell ill. "I've seen you walking with Cillian," Joseph continued. "Soon you might have a home of your own to manage. Now, come inside to the warmth." Joseph squeezed Anya's hand and opened the door.

As Anya stepped over the threshold, she was greeted warmly by the neighbors in the town, two kisses on each cheek as was the custom. When Anya reached the kitchen, she saw Mariloup standing in her mother's place at the stove. The candles in the room and fire in the hearth made Mariloup's chalky cheeks glow. Anya thought she would retch. She took a big breath, pushed the bile down and stole another glance at her father's smiling face. She wanted him to be happy. Her mother had wanted him to be happy. If Mariloup really made him happy, the least Anya could do was welcome her into their home. She walked toward her, noting the plum-colored silk of her dress. No mourning colors for Mariloup. And there was something else around her neck that Anya struggled to make sense of. Something that glowed in the light, that seemed to reflect all of the warmth of the fire and radiate it back onto Mariloup's face. Anya took a step closer.

Mariloup wore Liora's pearls.

Every day of her life, Liora had worn this double strand of champagne-colored pearls. Anya knew that there would be a diamond-crusted clasp on the back of Mariloup's starched-lace collar, three half-carat stones gracing the back. For a brief moment, Anya's sight turned black. Rage whipped through her veins like wildfire.

"Anya." Mariloup stepped toward her. "I hope you will accept my marriage to Joseph with grace." Anya couldn't speak; the anger choked her throat. Mariloup took a step toward her. "Your mother would want you to be ladylike about this." She placed a clammy palm on Anya's shoulder "She would expect it."

"Don't." Anya shook her hand off her shoulder. Looking around her, she swallowed hard and hissed. "Do not speak of my mother. She was… a saint… an angel. She held the magic of the earth in her hand. You…" Anya knew she should stop speaking, but words felt like they would burst inside her belly. "You are nothing but a used-up rotter," she hissed.

"Your mother was a witch!" Mariloup whispered, leaning in. Anya could smell her stale breath and turned her head. "She was not magical, she was loolah and almost ruined your father's reputation. And," Mariloup paused to look around the room, giving a mawkish smile to the guests, "She could not carry children. She failed your father."

Anya moved back as if she had been slapped. Tears sprung to her eyes. "How dare you!"

"She should have stayed on that Island with her sister, the other witch. The sooner that is all forgotten, the better."

"How dare you wear my mother's pearls?" Anya said, clenching her fists.

Mariloup clutched her neck protectively. "Your father gave these to me," she said. "As an engagement present. He said they are wedding pearls. They may be yours someday, if you ever get married."

"My father found those for HER. He spent days and nights at sea bringing in the fish and the lobster to have them strung, to pay for that clasp."

At the mention of the invaluable diamond clasp, Mariloup's face wrinkled into a sneer. One of the guests saw.

"Ladies," said the pastor, stepping gently in between the women. "The love you both bear for poor Joseph is admirable." He looked at Anya tenderly. "The sacrifice you make on his behalf for his happiness is truly a gift from God."

"Sacrifice?" Mariloup straightened.

"The sacrifice she has made to care for her father all these weeks until you came as a blessing to him," he said. "Now all will be well. You will both lead lives that you are meant to live." He laid a gentle hand on Anya's head and then turned to Mariloup. "It will be my honor to perform your wedding ceremony before this town and the eyes of God, ma'am." He nodded to them both and walked away.

"The life you were meant to lead, did you hear what Pastor said?" asked Mariloup. "You have several choices, more than I ever did. You can go to the Island, learn the… skills… of your aunt and your mother." She rolled her eyes.

"Their skills made the rings you wear so proudly on your hand. Their skills delivered your babies so many years ago," Anya glared at her.

Mariloup sucked air through her teeth at the mention of her grown children, the eldest of whom was born a mere three months after her first wedding. They left the village as soon as they married - and rarely returned. They didn't even write, although Mariloup posted weekly letters. The postage was a burden; her late husband had left her almost penniless. To her shame, she often had to take in washing; her eldest son sent very little. Their home was never happy, but her late husband had such a temper… she did what she could to keep

70

them safe but it was never enough. Mariloup clenched her teeth at the memory.

Anya smiled cruelly. "Where are your children now? Will they attend this... this wedding?" she spat.

What color warmed Mariloup's cheeks drained from her face. "I'm sure they will return for the wedding." Her voice was icy. "Speaking of marriage, if you do not wish to return to the Island, you could always marry Cillian." She tilted her head and squinted at Anya, unable to hide her smile. "Oh yes," she said. "I forgot. He hasn't asked you."

Anya had to physically stop herself from ripping the pearls of off Mariloup's neck. She pushed past the older woman and threw open the back door. "Firewood," she muttered to the guests standing by the sofa. Slamming the door behind her, Anya stepped out into the snowy night.

CHAPTER SIXTEEN

It was scandalous to be seen at Cillian's house at any time, but being seen there after the sun had long set was unforgivable. Anya couldn't think, and when she could, she didn't care. They would be married soon anyway; they would leave this place. She could forget her father's betrayal. How could he have loved her mother? How, if he could welcome that woman into their hearth so quickly? All because her mother could not bear children and that hag could? Mariloup had birthed children, but she had driven them away. They left the village the first chance they could. And the pearls... around Mariloup's neck!

Anya continued marching up the snowy path. Fury ran fiercely through her veins so that she could not feel the snow as it seeped through her boots.

When she arrived at Cillian's small, ramshackle cabin, the snow had soaked through her stockings. She knocked on the door hard with the flat of her hand. "Cillian," she called, not caring if anyone heard. They'd be married soon enough. "Cillian!"

Fast footsteps approached and Cillian inched the door open. "My God, Anya!" he said. He pulled his shirt closed over his chest. "What are you doing?"

"I'm sorry," Anya stammered. "I had to leave. Have I woken you?"

Cillian looked behind him in the room. "Anya, people will see you," he said, taking a step out into the cold. "People will talk and then what will you do? You'll have no options."

"I don't care about any of that," Anya said. "You said we'll be together; you said we can make a life in Montreal." She shivered. "I'm so cold, Cillian. Please, let me in."

Behind the door, a voice called out. Anya stared at him. Swallowing hard, she pushed past him and crossed the threshold of the cabin.

Sitting by the fire was a voluptuous young woman Anya knew from the village. Cillian often had women sighing at him from afar, but they were usually the older mothers of the town who knew and loved the music he played. Most young girls were not so bold. This one, though, often approached him in the square or after church, glaring and scuttling away when she saw Anya coming.

"Hannah." Anya breathed. "Does your mother know you're here?"

Hannah lifted her chin. "I was having harp lessons." She lifted a harp off the floor. "I take a lesson every week."

Anya walked slowly toward Hannah, determined not to let the betrayal she felt show on her face. Hannah was full-figured for such a young woman, but then, her father had wealth. She was fed well. Her breasts bloomed out of her dress, which had been unbuttoned from the neck. She leaned over Hannah and looked over her very slowly. "Harp lesson," Anya said quietly.

"Anya, it's not what it seems," Cillian said, walking over to Anya and attempting an embrace. Anya stepped back wildly.

"She's a child, Cillian!"

"I'm fifteen!" Hannah protested. Cillian looked pained and gestured for her be quiet.

"We were just having a harp lesson. The fire was so hot, and while we were playing, it became too much, uncomfortable..."

"So you unbuttoned her dress and your shirt, I see. You wanted to see the teats of your prize cow!" Hannah covered her chest and began to cry. Anya turned to her. "Go home, Hannah. Cover up and go home before anyone sees you." Hannah looked to Cillian, eyes wide with tears. "Now!" Anya yelled. Hannah hastily packed her harp and cloak and ran from the cabin.

"Anya, I promise, nothing happened."

"Nothing?" Anya asked. Her voice was hollow. She was barely able to breathe, but her eyes were dry.

"Not everything, not the main thing," Cillian said, color rising to his cheeks. You're the only one for me.

We'll go to Montreal, we'll make a life, as you said. You're the only one I love."

At the word love, something broke inside Anya. It was the first time he had ever told her he loved her. The first time in two years, the first time he had said the word "love." Never had he said the word – not during all those times she lay down for him, and given all she had to him, believing that love lay beneath his promises.

She reached back and slapped him across the face with all her strength. Then she turned and walked back out into the snow.

CHAPTER SEVENTEEN

It had been a week since Anya returned to the Island. had been on the Island for a week. She told Airmed about Mariloup, about Cillian, she had cried until her eyes ached. Each day, Airmed woke her with the sunrise and worked her hard. Anya learned the prayers, labored in the forge, polished the stones. In the evenings, Anya and Airmed would stand by the stove mixing herbs and making medicines and teas. Not a word was said about Cillian, and Airmed noted with relief when Anya began to quietly wash her monthly rags.

Each day when the sun was fully in the sky, Anya sat in silent reflection, breathing in the air. Airmed instructed her to contemplate to draw from the powers of the earth, feeling the strength come through the cold ground to her legs and torso. She was to breathe in the emanation of the air, the wind, the direction, etc. to give her soul wings to fly. A candle rested in her hand, and Airmed instructed her to stare into the flames, seeing the secrets that lay there. Lastly, Anya was to catch snowflakes on her sleeve, studying the shapes that appeared in lines and eddies, created magic that shimmered for anyone who took the time to look. Airmed asked her what the lesson was of the snowflakes disappearance.

Anya wrote all of this down and soon, Airmed asked more of her. She told Anya to harness these powers. She instructed her niece to blow gently at the last leaves on the beech trees and watch them fall. She taught her to reach a hand out to the sea and watch the waves grow stronger. Anya would breathe deeply, root to the earth, beckoning the waves with her hand to make them grow, pushing them away to calm the waters.

One day at dusk, Airmed led Anya out to the bay. She unclasped the stone necklace from around her niece's neck and placed it her hand, stone against her palm. "If you want to see the future, look," the older women said. "Within yourself." Anya stepped closer to the water and closed her eyes.

Air traveled down through her lungs, her belly expanding to take in as much as she could. Placing the jewel in her cupped hands, she planted her feet on the cold ground. Concentrated on breathing, steadily, deeply. Evenly.

The darkness behind her eyelids began to flicker with light. A chill floated up through her chest and lifted her onto her toes and she swayed.

"Stand firm."

Anya heard Airmed's voice as if it were a mile away, but she obeyed. Still breathing deeply, she straightened her hips, and rolled her shoulders back and down. Planted her feet, this time without moving.

Anya began to feel light – the magic swayed inside her but her body remained strong. The bits of light spiraled and took shape: pillars of smoke that rose against a clear, cold sky. Anya felt whisked across a plane, a wet wind whipping at her hair. The stone in her hand became her heart, tied to a string, beating, strong. Her heart, dropped into the water, into the waves. A monstrous shape below, screams and ungodly waves. A flash of green, a horrid flash of red. Without knowing that she spoke, she whispered a name.

A field of swaying sweet grasses came into her vision – towering sparse pine trees, white flaking birches, their leaves glittering in the air. A pang of hunger ripped at her gut. The heart beat in her hands. She placed it on the grass, and the blood flowed in rivers on the ground, swirling and solidifying into stone. The same stones that made her aunt's house: granite and sandstone.

Now she was swirling in eddies of lace and silk the color of sunshine. Golden thread wound around her fingers, curls, softer than lambs wool. The bright sky over the unfamiliar shore turned a sickening shade of green, clouds blowing toward her. She ran into the woodland, seeking the shelter of the trees but their branches reached out and stung her face – grasses twisted around her ankles.

She fell. Mud smeared her tear-soaked cheek – her muscles were frozen- she could not move.

A howl emerged from the depths of the Earth – a second cry came flying across the wind, wrapping around her, around the vines tangled at her feet, clawing at the scratches on her cheek, until their sound was unbearable and she was engulfed.

Her heart. Her heart beat in a light-filled room. She could feel it, feel it beating in four different places- in the four cardinal directions. She reached out to touch it – to grasp it back, but it flew, laughing, beyond her mind. And music, swirling around her so that she spun, hair lifting from her neck, body lifted in the air. Music played on strings, silky and deep. She knew the song, knew it in her mind, and she reached up to touch the stars, each twinkling a note floating across a midnight sky. Anya opened her throat and tipped her head back to the expanse, joining her voice to the tune. As she joined the final note, the dark sky of her mind seemed to burst with light and she expanded within it in a million streams of light.

Her hands were on the cold, wet earth; her back arched and aching. Anya opened her eyes. Snow fell and the midmorning sun above the Island gave its meager light. Anya shifted off of her knees and rubbed her back. She looked up to find Airmed staring. "I heard a song," Anya said.

"You sang the tune," Airmed answered. Her brows furrowed as she looked at her niece.

"It was…" Anya struggled to find the words, struggled to find her breath. "I was in the sky… I was the sky. And the song was one… one I have always known."

"I know," Airmed said.

Anya stared at the sea, trying in vain to bring the tune back to her memory, back to her lips. She hummed a few notes and then as if by the wind, the tune slipped from her mind and out with the waves. "It must've been a song of the Old Ones?" Anya asked, looking at her aunt. "That's why I can't recall it now. It exists only beyond the veil?"

"It is a common pub song," Airmed said shortly. "'The Apron,' I believe it's called."

"Mason's Apron," Anya said, sighing. "My mother sings… would sing it all the time." The tune came to her now, with a stab of pain.

"Of course she would." Airmed shook her head and stepped over to the younger woman. "Goddess forbid she teach her only daughter the Old Songs." Airmed extended her hand and helped Anya rise. "Ah well. Your jewelry making is extraordinary and your embroidery surpasses my own. I suppose it is too much to hope that…"

"What?" Anya asked.

"That you could be the next Diviner. The seer of visions. That you might see beyond the toils of this life and tell of the future." Airmed patted Anya's hand before dropping it and leading them briskly away. When they returned to the stone house, Airmed paused and bored her gaze into

Anya's. "You must practice, though. You must not be afraid to reach for what is beyond the present circumstance."

By the end of the third week, Anya could sweep her hand to the night sky and wash away the cloud cover, making stars shine brightly. The first time she did this, Airmed gasped aloud. "You are stronger than any woman in our family has ever been," she said. She stepped back and bowed her head slightly in one graceful gesture. "You can do so much good in this world, Anya. You just need a bit more practice."

"Which I could have if you would let me stay here," Anya said, repeating the request she made daily.

Airmed shook her head.

"You have to return for the wedding," she said. "You have to honor your father. It's only right. You are his only child. You cannot disgrace him."

Anya sighed. "Can I return right after?"

Airmed took her hands gently. "You mustn't let them think you are spending all your time on this Island. You must live your life. It's what your mother would have wanted. You may return, but only for a fortnight. We will make plans." Airmed returned to the cupboard and brought out a small velvet bag. "You have learned the secret of the stones. You have performed the Ceremony. It is time for you to have a set of your own. Perhaps you can go to Montreal, on your own. And perhaps, if you are ready, I will give you the Book."

Anya's heart leapt in her chest. The Book contained all the meanings of the stones, both scientific and spiritual, all the herbal knowledge and recipes. All the prayers. Airmed had been unsure of how old it was; she had brought it with her from Scotland. The first several entries were in Gaelic.

"You must leave tomorrow," Airmed said firmly. A smile drew at her lips. "The wind will be at your back though," she said. "She always will."

CHAPTER EIGHTEEN

When Anya returned to the house, neither her father nor Mariloup was there. She stoked the flames in the hearth and tried not to think about the suffocating scent of Mariloup's perfume that pervaded the air of the house.

She hung up her cloak and reached up for the tea, sprinkling sweet lavender and mint leaves in the hand painted teapot, and placed her favorite teacup on the counter beside it. Just as Anya put the kettle over the flames of the stove, there was a sharp rap on the door. Smoothing her dress, Anya went to answer it. The person on the other side continued rapping furiously as Anya crossed the room. She turned the handle and Cillian burst into the foyer.

"You've made a fool of me!" he shouted, rounding on her.

"What do you mean?" Anya asked, backing up against the trestle table.

Cillian dug in his coat pocket and produced the golden stone he had chosen at his Ceremony. He waved it in her face. "This... this ROCK!" he yelled, clenching it now in his fist. "It's not gold, it's just a rock."

"Stop shouting," Anya said firmly. "Sit down."

"Stop shouting? Stop shouting?? Don't you tell me what to do, you worthless – you woman! I took this godforsaken rock to the jeweler in Montreal – I went to Montreal! Do you know what that cost me?"

"Why would you take that anywhere?" Anya asked, backing up more so that the wide wooden table was between her and Cillian. "It's your spirit stone."

"My spirit stone," Cillian hissed, the color draining from his face. "This was supposed to get me to Montreal. Get my life started, get me out of this godforsaken village. And you know what it is?"

Anya shook her head.

"It's pyrite," Cillian's voice was deadly as he leaned over the table and shoved the rock in her eyeline again. He looked at it and his face twisted. "Fool's gold!" Anya ducked and covered her head as Cillian threw the stone across the table. It passed into the kitchen and smashed into the teacup. The cup shattered to the ground.

Cillian's eyes went wide but the fury did not disperse. He looked at Anya. "I thought you loved me," he said. "I thought that's why you gave yourself to me." Walking slowly, he began to round the table where Anya stood. She didn't move. "Over and over in those woods, you showed me that you loved me. I thought myself so lucky that there was no baby…" He grabbed her arm. She tried to yank it away, but he held firm. "We were supposed to have a life," he said. A tear ran down his cheek. Anya stood shocked and silent. "You were supposed to have a life with me in Montreal, and interesting life, and now…" He squeezed her arm harder and she held his gaze. Finally, he gave a shuddering sigh and released her. "You've broken me, Anya. You've made me a fool." He looked past her to the shattered teacup and chunk of pyrite that lay on the floor. "I thought you loved me. And I loved you. But now I know who you really are. A woman. A barren woman who made a fool of me."

CHAPTER NINETEEN

The kettle screeched, but Anya didn't hear it. All her mind could hear was the sound of the teacup shattering. She thought of what might have happened if she hadn't ducked. Had Cillian meant that for her face?

For several minutes, Anya stood frozen, staring at the door that Cillian had stomped through, slamming it behind him. There was snow drift on the floor. Without thinking, Anya reached up and gingerly rubbed her arm. It was throbbing. She unbuttoned her dress and shrugged the sleeve down. Four ugly dark bruises dotted her skin where his fingers had dug in.

Water boiled out of the kettle and shrieked as it hit the stove top. She shuddered and hurried over to the stove, pulling the kettle from the flames. Grabbing a broom, she swept up the remains of the teacup and threw it in the bin. Tears stung her eyes as she saw the delicate, hand-painted flowers on the cup, now in pieces. Her mother had painted that, just as she had painted the pink rosebuds on the teapot.

The piece of pyrite shone from the light of the stove fire and Anya lifted it from where it lay. Her throat clenched. What was this? Pyrite was not among any stone she had studied, nor any she had polished. Was this trickery? Anya's heart fluttered in her chest. She had not known her aunt to be anything but honest. Brutally so. Write, she thought quickly. She would write Airmed. If she hurried, the letter could be put in the evening mail call that went out to the island.

Anya pocketed the pyrite and made for the desk.

CHAPTER TWENTY

Mariloup and Anya had had a row so big the night before the wedding that Joseph had to get involved. Mariloup had been looking for Liora's double strand of pearls and couldn't find it. She immediately accused Anya of taking them, to which Anya replied that they were Liora's and would never belong to her.

Mariloup shouted so fiercely that Joseph came in from outside.

"What on earth is happening?" he asked, stepping between Mariloup and Anya.

"Your daughter has stolen the pearls!" Mariloup burst into tears. Joseph frowned.

"Anya will be your daughter as well, come tomorrow," Joseph said, patting her arm. "Perhaps you could learn to speak with each other in a kinder manner." Turning to Anya, he asked gently, "Do you know where that necklace is?"

"I was raised well enough not to go into your bedroom without permission, Father. I assume it is in

Mother's jewelry case. Mother's," she said, throwing a look at Mariloup.

"Raised well enough," Mariloup muttered, rubbing her wet nose with an embroidered handkerchief. "You were raised like a – "

"Mari." Joseph's tone was leaden. "I advise you not to finish that sentence. Now, Anya. I will ask you again. Do you know where the pearls are?"

Anya looked up at her father, tears beginning to gather in her eyes. She did not know. She did not know how her life had fallen into so much disarray that her mother's precious double strand had been lost. She did not know why Airmed would not write her back. It had been a week.

Joseph saw her tears and put a strong hand on her arm. The pain from bruises Cillian left was still fresh and Anya winced and pulled away. Joseph tsked and put his hand on his forehead.
Finally, he said, "Anya, I'm disappointed. You were raised with much more grace than you are displaying now. Your words, your actions shame me."

He leaned into Mariloup, who was still weeping theatrically. "She will be your daughter," he said firmly. "The only one you will have in the village. Find a way to care for her." Joseph set his chin and marched out of the house.

Mariloup dabbed her eyes. She turned toward Anya and shook her head.

"Your father is right," she said. "My children have left. And you are the daughter of this house. But I will be the mistress of this house. Beginning tomorrow at dawn. You will need to accept this."

Anya said nothing, moving toward the stove to set the kettle on. She put tea leaves in the pink teapot and tried to avoid feeling Mariloup's stare bore into her back.

"I see," Mariloup said. "Your silence is your defiance. And your father will say nothing to your nothingness. That's as may be. Well, Miss Anya. You may rule the roost tonight, but tomorrow that will change. Tomorrow you will do as I say. You will help me run this house as it should have been run, and you will not brook or question anything I say or do."

Anya looked at her and poured the hot water into the teapot.

"Tea?" Anya asked.

Mariloup shook her head. "You are not a bad child. I have a sense that if you put your mind to it, you may listen to me. And if you do, we may have a peaceful time of it."

"Did that work with your other children?" Anya sipped her tea. She knew it was cruel, and it would pain her father to hear her say it, but ...

Mariloup sucked in her breath and snatched her cloak off the hook. "Tomorrow, my girl," she said. "Tomorrow we will change things."

Anya kept her gaze as she marched out of the house. At the sound of the door latch, she wept.

CHAPTER TWENTY-ONE

The wedding ceremony was brief. Cillian played as had been planned. Anya had to watch him play throughout the service, hearing that music flood her ears. She was determined not to cry, but even more determined to catch Cillian's eye. Cillian did not glance her way.

Mariloup wore her finest emerald silk. No necklace. After the incident with the pearls, Joseph went to the jeweler in Montreal bought an enormous opal brooch set in copper. Mariloup adored the heavy piece, pinned it right on her throat, causing her starched lace collar to sag.

It was Anya's task to ready the home for the wedding breakfast. After the final wedding hymn, she embraced her father and kissed Mariloup on both cheeks with as much grace as such could muster.

Anya put on her cloak. She must catch Cillian before he left, and she knew it would take him a minute to pack his harp. She had to explain what happened, had to apologize. Opening the door to the asp, she saw her.

Hannah. The light from the window lit up her blond curls, which bounced playfully as she laughed with Cillian.

At the sound of the door, Cillian looked up. "Sweetheart, can you give us a moment?" Hannah stuck out her lower lip. "Please?" he asked, kissing her hand. Hannah blushed and nodded, throwing a look to Anya as she sidled out of the room.

"I didn't know," Anya said.

Cillian stood up. "Anya," he began, his face pale.

"I didn't know it was pyrite," she continued. "I thought it was a new stone. Something I hadn't seen. Something special. I never imagined you thought it was gold."

"I should never have come to your home like that," Cillian said. "That was a mistake. When I think about it, I want to…"

"Cillian!" Joseph's stern voice boomed into the room. "I believe I owe you payment."

Cillian's face crumpled. "I couldn't possibly accept, Sir. Please let it be my wedding gift."

Joseph looked hard at the younger man. "I would not accept. I must pay you. Especially with the news I have so recently heard. My congratulations." Joseph extended his hand with several large bills. "Let this be ended here." Joseph held the younger man's gaze for a long moment before turning to his daughter.

"Anya, let us finish this business as men. Please go attend to Mariloup."

"But Father, we were finishing our conversation."

"Anya, please." An unfamiliar edge snuck into Joseph's voice. "Now."

Cillian looked at her desperately, but Anya was unwilling to start a fight with her father. She had a feeling there would be enough opportunity for that later. She turned and walked back into the chapel.

Mariloup's voice rang through the open hall as she stood by Olivia O'Toole, one of her few friends. "Well, that's where they are. I've packed them for the trip. I won't have her taking what is mine. She's a child and I won't have it."

"She's a young woman," said Olivia. "And the grief is still new for her. Perhaps the necklace will bring her some comfort. Joseph has you for comfort but Mariloup, who does she have? Especially now." Mariloup scoffed and shook her head. "Joseph loves you," Olivia said. "He loves his daughter. He's a good man."

"That's as may be," Mariloup said. "But she will have to find something to do. I won't have her on the Island with that aunt – "

"What about my aunt?" Anya said, stepping out from the hallway.

Mariloup straightened. "I don't think it's fitting for you to live with your aunt on the Island, Anya."

"Neither does she," Anya said.

"Well, soon I'm sure it will be your turn at the altar," Olivia O'Toole said, smiling at Anya. "Everyone knows you've been walking out with Cillian. Married to a harpist, how exciting!"

Anya looked pained. Olivia looked between the women. Mariloup looked pained as well.

"Oh, he hasn't asked," she said. "He will. Darling, they always do."

Mariloup looked out past the open door where Hannah stood in the sunshine. "Anya will be happy living with us at the house for the time being. I'm sure she will serve as a dutiful daughter should until the time comes for her to marry."

Anya threw a look at Mariloup so full of disgust that the elder woman took a step back. "Serve? I will never serve you," she hissed under her breath.

"Anya Lyon," said Olivia, "You were not brought up to speak like this! What would your father say?"

Anya heard her father's voice in the hall. His conversation with Cillian must be ending. She would go find him. Suffering his rebuke would be better than watching her father and Mariloup embrace yet again.

Anya turned to the older women. "Thank you for coming to my father's wedding, Mrs. O'Toole," she said formally. "I will see you at our home for the wedding breakfast." She began to walk away when Mariloup stepped in her path.

"Don't embarrass yourself," she said. "Don't shame yourself further," she said.

"Please move," Anya said. "I have to talk to Cillian."

"You have no business with Cillian Hughes," Mariloup said firmly. "I have told you to stay here."

"You have no right to tell me whether to stay or go!"

"I have every right. I am your mother now; God help us both. And I tell you to stay. If you go to him, you bring shame to yourself and to us."

"He's a brilliant musician! He will go to Montreal; he will make a career."

"With Hannah Balfour."

The color drained from Anya's face.

"He will go to Montreal with Hannah Balfour," Mariloup repeated. "He will take her as his wife. Not you."

"That is… you are so cruel," Anya said, blood raging through her veins. "Why would you-"

"Stop." Mariloup put her hand out. "Stop this now." Anya looked as if she would strike her. "Compose yourself," Mariloup said, stepping toward Anya and placing a tentative hand on the younger woman's shoulder. "Cillian has proposed to Hannah Balfour. While you were on the Island. Some say there is a bairn on the way. These things happen." Mariloup looked her up and down. "Well, for most women. In any case, he is not for you anymore.

CHAPTER TWENTY-TWO

Anya ran from the church, despair clutching at her heart. The house came into view and already she was homesick. It wasn't her house anymore. Not after today. As she crossed the threshold, ice ran through her veins. She knew that after today, she would never set foot in this house again.

She ran up to her bedroom and snatched an old carpet bag from under the bed. Throwing it open, she tossed in her few dresses and linens. Anya had a few pieces of stone jewelry that her mother had given to her; those she wrapped carefully in embroidered handkerchiefs. Grabbing her hairbrush and hand mirror, she took a breath. Snow fell hard outside her window and Anya knew it would cause the wedding party to delay.

The pearls.

Her mother's pearls. They belonged to her; they should go with her. It wasn't stealing; Mariloup had no right to them. What had Mariloup been saying in the hallway of the church? Something about her bag. Anya hesitated for only a moment before racing across the hall. Joseph and Mariloup's suitcases were set neatly by the stairs. She flipped the larger suitcase on its back and undid the clasp, ruffling through the dark gowns and plain linens until she felt the velvet box. She pulled it out and lifted the lid.

The double strand of champagne-colored pearls shone in the weak winter sunlight. Anya carefully opened the diamond clasp and fastened the pearls around her neck, tucking them under her dress. They were cold against her skin.

If she was to reach the boat before they returned, she only had a few moments. She scrambled up and tripped over Mariloup's suitcase. From a small pocket on the side, an envelope fell onto the floor.

Just one word was written on it: "Eilidh"

Anya picked it up. It looked like a letter and it had been opened and then resecured. Her aunt had written back. Mariloup must have read the letter. And hidden it.

If Anya had any remaining thoughts that she could live under the same roof as this woman, they vanished. Tucking the letter into the pocket of her cloak, she lifted her wet skirts and ran down the stairs. The bells on the horses' tack tinkled outside. They were almost here. The thought of not saying goodbye to her father tore at her heart, but she might hurt him more with the words she would say if she saw Mariloup again. The light shone in the window and sparkled on the golden spout of the teapot.

Her mother's teapot. Liora had brewed tea in that pot every day of Anya's memory. Tea that cured colds, tea that settled stomachs, tea that simply added to the warmth of the hearthside. And the solid gold spout was valuable. If Anya needed something…

Voices rang through the snow. It was now or never. Anya raced across the house, grabbed the teapot and hid it under her cloak.

The front door opened and let in the sounds of merriment and laughter. No one heard the quiet latch of the back door.

CHAPTER TWENTY-THREE

Anya reached the shoreline as the sun rose to the apex of the sky. She looked on the path behind her; no one had followed. Taking the letter out of her pocket, she untied the string and unfolded the paper. Her aunt's spidery script flowed across the page.

"Dear Eilidh,

I hope that you will accept the marriage between your father and Mariloup with as much grace as a woman in our family would be expected to show. Mariloup might have been one of us, but for the tragedies that befell her.

You will become a woman of great substance when you are finished with your training. Your skills in forging already surpass my own, and your ability to communicate with the Spirit surpasses everything I will ever do. If you continue to practice, you will be able to see what others cannot see. You will be able to see what lies ahead in the world and in the lives of those around you. In doing so, you can help them. But you must practice. And pray. For you are far from achieving that skill.

It concerned me greatly that you cannot see who Cillian is. That man is a musician of great skill, yes, but great foolishness also. He can play the songs of the Good Neighbors, but does not respect their power. Nor can he wield it. He does a dangerous act when he plays those notes. He simply weaves the magic into the air with no regard of the consequences.

And Eilidh, there are consequences in life.

The nine stones of the Old Lake were set before Cillian Hughes for him to choose.

I also set a tenth stone. The luminescent golden stone he chose was not gold at all, but pyrite. Pyrite is a stone used for protection. I was correct in thinking that it might protect you from this man. He chose the false gold rather than any of our nine sacred stones. He is false, Eilidh. No doubt he will attempt to sell the rock as gold ore, bringing himself mighty shame. It is my hope that this happens only after you untangle yourself from him. He is false, Eilidh."

The wind whipped around Anya, pulling her hair out of the elaborate chignon she had pinned for the wedding. Airmed had not made a fool out of Cillian, she had made a fool out of her! How could she had done this? Why couldn't Airmed have simply spoken her thoughts about Cillian to Anya? Anya could have explained – could have told her that Cillian did need the money, that anyone needed money to start a successful life. He was talented. By Airmed's treachery, Cillian was driven into the arms of that moneyed brat Hannah. A sob escaped Anya's lips. Now there was no chance. Cillian would marry Hannah. Hannah would bear his child.

Cillian's child, who would have his curls, his deep sable eyes.

She crushed the letter in the palm of her hand. There was more, but Anya couldn't read another word. She would go to the Island, now, and answer Airmed's letter in person.

CHAPTER TWENTY-FOUR

The north wind guided the boat toward the Island. Anya paddled fiercely. The carpet bag was nestled underneath her legs. The teapot was still there. In one piece.

The tea. What tea had Airmed given her? What had it done to her, to Cillian? When she had finished throwing her fury in Airmed's face, she would force the older woman to tell her. And then...

What?

What would she do? Stay on the Island? She couldn't imagine living with Airmed after her betrayal. She couldn't imagine finding forgiveness in what her aunt had done. Or trust. And besides, Airmed had been very clear: Anya could not stay on the island. She had to live her life.

But what life was there left for her to live?

The sun bloomed from underneath the snowclouds, lighting her way. It would only be a quarter of an hour until the canoe struck the rocky shore. Anya gulped back tears. If she was going to confront her aunt, she had better have a plan. For Airmed would surely know she was coming. She always did.

Anya dug the letter out of her pocket. There was one more page.

Eilidh, your place is in the World. You can be a woman of great power in the world. You can accomplish what your mother could not accomplish. Your abilities are stronger than hers ever were. Cillian would have impeded you in this, so he was sent on a different path. If you can swallow your pride and serve your village, you can accomplish what I was unable to accomplish on this Island. I thought the villagers would come to me, would respect the gifts I had to give. I thought they would join us. Instead, they gave only slander. I tell you now what you must do: You must stay in the village until your father and Mariloup return. You must continue to come to me every fortnight, to learn and obey exactly what I tell you. You must find the strength to live in your home, for you shall not live with me. It could be that Hannah will need your help and our skills with the bairn. You could prove yourself in that way.

Tears welled up in Anya's eyes. The bairn. Mariloup. She could not face it. Bile rose in her throat and suddenly she retched. Leaning over the side of the small boat, she vomited into the waves.

Anya looked to the sky. To the north, the Island became clearer.

Obey. She must obey if she were to visit. There was no shelter there, no home, but she must obey. She must learn to help those who shattered her heart, must learn to forget betrayal.

She looked back at the mainland. The steeple of the church was barely visible in the sky. There was no one in the village for her now that Cillian was lost to her. No one but her father. And he belonged to Mariloup.

Anya looked to the sky and let out a keening wail. She let go of the oars, folded her head in her arms against the side of the boat and sobbed.

A gust of wind propelled the boat toward the Island. Sea water splashed on the letter in her hand. There were still more words to be read.

Anya felt the teapot bounce gently against her leg. Her mother's pearls rested warmly on her throat. Her pearls now.

Her life.

Suddenly, an emptying. Everything, every pain, every anger seemed to drain from her very bones. She was empty, barren.

But she was alive.

She took a breath. An oak leaf floated on the waves and she lifted it and set it in her lap. It was impossible that there would be an oak leaf on the sea so far into the winter.

And yet.

Anya raised her eyes in the direction of the leaf and saw a white feather. She lifted the oars and gave a few gentle paddles. Soon, the feather was in her lap as well. The sun seemed to gently float in the sky and she looked toward it.

West.

The great City was to the west. Cillian's city. He would not go now, not with Hannah and the child.

But she could go.

Anya felt a sparkle through her veins. A brush of holy air. The crossing over open waters would be impossible, but if she stayed on the shoreline, if she called to the Spirit for help... A larger fishing town was so close and from there, she could find a way to secure passage on a bigger boat.

Gingerly, she picked up the paddles and turned the canoe westward. She looked toward the Island. Airmed would be watching, would surely see. She might use strength that Anya did not yet understand to come after her, to force her to return.

But Airmed did not have a boat.

Anya still grasped the letter between her palm and the handle of the oar. She looked at it and compared it to the leaf and feather in her lap. The sun shone warm upon her face. Anya looked up into its brightness and then, throwing her arm out, cast the letter with its unread pages into the sea. Anya set her course for the West.

PART II

CHAPTER TWENTY-FIVE

Anya walked down to the pier, rubbing her hands against the late winter chill. Her fingers were sore from the piecework she embroidered seven days a week, but the linens brought in a decent income. It paid enough for her to have a room in a boarding house close enough to the sea that she could walk safely there each day at twilight to feel the sun on her face.

The voyage on the ship had been terrifying, exhilarating. It was the first time Anya had done anything alone besides canoe to the Island. Thinking of the canoe, she swallowed hard. It had been a bitter pill to sell the hand-carved boat to pay for passage on the steamer. But she had been tough and negotiated a good price, enough that she had some savings and had not needed to sell anything else. The teapot sat safely perched on her bureau. The pearls nestled at her throat.

Agnes Carre, the landlady, had promised Anya that in the spring, she could take a small plot in the back garden and plant some herbs. Anya walked along the cobbled street peeking into the windows of shops. Perhaps some would carry seeds soon.

Seagulls began to caw as Anya approached the pier. She heard the low bellow of the big ship's horns, and the mixture of French, English, and Gaelic as the stevedores unloaded the cargo. Looking around to ensure that no one was watching, Anya began to softly sing. She had found that if she didn't practice the old Gaelic tunes from Airmed and her mother, they slipped from her memory as quickly as the morning mist. As Mrs. Carre said it was unladylike to sing in the boarding house, Anya sang the songs quietly to herself as she stepped onto the pier.

She scanned the docks and looked for a spot where boats were tied up and empty. Turning down one dock that looked abandoned but for an old sailboat tied up, she took one last look to assure herself she was really alone. Running her palm gently down the salty, damp wood of the railing as she walked, she began to surrender to the pleasure of the music. The notes twisted and sparkled into the air as Anya sang the old, melancholy tunes. She looked out to the horizon and saw the darkness of night beginning to rise in the East. The East. Toward her home. Toward her family. Well. Anya straightened up and looked pointedly at the clouds. It wasn't her home anymore. She had no home.

A small skiff lay anchored just to the south of the docks. The sound of a woman singing caused Liam Leighton to set down the lobster trap in the hull of the

boat, soaking his boots. Taking a small swig of the bottle
of beer he had brought with him, he listened. That
song… he had heard it before. He felt it in his bones.

Liam looked towards Montreal, if he could
possibly see the outdoor concert where the woman must
be singing. It would be worth coming in for this.

A sharp pain in his ankle caused him to jump,
spilling the beer. Liam swore gently under his breath and
looked down. A lobster had stuck out his claw and
pinched him. Liam moved his foot away and smiled
ruefully. "You'll be in the pot soon enough," he said to
the lobster. "Fight your fight while you can." He
carefully picked up the lobster cage and moved it away
from his legs. When he looked up, he saw a beam of
sunshine illuminating the source of the music. A slight
young woman stood on the edge of the dock, her arms
draped over the side of the railing. Dark auburn hair was
swept into a chignon at the nape of her neck. A plaid
woolen shawl was draped across her shoulders. Without
thinking, Liam picked up the paddles of his skiff and
propelled himself slowly toward the dock. The woman's
perfect bow lips open and shut gently and she closed her
eyes as she soared to a higher note, spinning the music as
it descended. Liam was entranced. He paddled the skiff
almost up to the dock. Her indigo skirts were crusted
with the salt of the sea air and her boots were fine, but for
a small hole at the tip. Her toes must constantly be cold,
he thought.

Liam looked up at her face. Her skin was golden even in winter, and smooth as silk. Luminous brown eyes opened up and gazed out at the horizon. There was a sorrow behind them, a yearning, and Liam wondered if she wandered to the pier to have a moment's escape from a surly husband. She had to be married, he thought. Pearls like that were never given to somebody's daughter. Liam watched as she withdrew an object from her pocket and rolled it around in her palm. She closed her eyes and took a slow, deliberate breath in. She let it out slowly, placing her free hand on her stomach. Liam wondered if she carried a child. She seemed so young. He leaned forward in the skiff, careful not to make the wooden boards of the boat creak, trying to see if a gold wedding band glinted on her finger.

Suddenly, the lobster reached its claw out and knocked the bottle of beer over where it clattered all over the boat.

Anya gasped as she jumped back. How long had he been floating there?

"Sorry," Liam called up. At the sound of his voice, Anya startled and dropped the stone she had been holding.

In one swift movement, Liam stretched himself up and with one boot on the seat of the skiff, reached up and caught the stone. "Got it!" he said, grinning and falling back into the boat.

Tears of embarrassment and fury welled up in Anya's eyes.

Gripping the stone as he regained his balance, Liam righted the beer bottle and the lobster cage. When he looked up to greet the woman, he only saw the flash of indigo silk rushing off the dock.

"Wait!" he called. "Miss!" Noticing the stone was attached to a chain, he wound it around his palm and called again. "Miss, come back! I caught it! I have it!"

But Anya was long gone.

CHAPTER TWENTY-SIX

Anya didn't return to the pier. Furious with herself for being so careless and mortified a fisherman would have seen her in her most private moments, would have heard her sing the old songs... the thought made her want to fold in on herself and disappear. It was enough that Cillian... her throat tightened all these months later at just the thought of him. Still, Anya forced herself to finish the thought. It was penance. It was enough that Cillian Hughes had seen every part of her, knew every secret. She had let him in and it wasn't enough. He was still willing to let her go after one mistake. She still didn't know whether the mistake belonged to him, or to herself. It didn't matter, really. She would never let anyone else see her for who she was. It was that simple. In that way, she would be safe.

The thought of losing her Spirit Stone was devastating. It was the last connection she had to her family, to the ways she was trying to learn, trying to maintain. Her mother had been there the day she had chosen the stone at her Ceremony. She was only a toddler. It was Liora's fingers who forged the setting and carved in the ancient, intricate symbols. Liora's hands who braided the chain. And now the whole thing was in the hands of another fisherman, another man who wanted what he wanted, and would take it without a second thought.

Day in and day out, she embroidered handkerchiefs, linen shifts, bedding, any work that the factory would give her. Her craftsmanship was exceptional, and Mr. Porcher, the foreman, knew it. What's more, he knew that Anya knew it, and so she was paid a bit more that the pittance he usually allowed for embroidery. However, she was aware that he made ten times profit than what he paid her. Well, she had had enough. Enough of the stuffy boarding house, enough of mending clothes, enough of her boots with the holes that let in every droplet of wet. Anya had discreetly inquired and found that if she took in work on her own, she could make twice as much as Mr. Porcher was paying. The problem was, taking in embroidery from the factory was consistent work. Anya had decided that the best thing would be to confront Mr. Porcher and ask him for more payment. She would tell him what she had discovered. Anya jutted her pointed chin in the mirror and pursed her full mouth. She straightened the pearl necklace, took up the pile of embroidered linen, and marched out of the door.

CHAPTER TWENTY-SEVEN

Liam placed his Stetson on his head and looked in the mirror. His posting as a Mountie made his chest swell with pride. He knew he looked handsome in his red woolen uniform with the black epaulets outlined in creamy white. He only wished his mother could see him. His bright blue eyes clouded for a moment thinking of her face.

"Liam!" A booming voice resounded from the next room and confident footsteps strode forward. "You will be late to your post." Liam's father was even taller than he was, and had the same wide-set eyes, sharp cheekbones, and full build. He reached out enormous hands and adjusted the brim. He clapped Liam hard on the shoulder. "Go on."

Liam gave a crisp nod and turned on his heel. He had hoped that being chosen for the Mounties would impress his father. What he really preferred was fishing, the freedom of the open sea, the oneness between himself and the waves. At sea, you didn't control the world, you respected it. The power of nature was beyond any amount of control man could impose. And that felt right to Liam.

Walking down the cobblestone street, he remembered a time when he was young and his family had visited relatives in the country. Liam had gotten to help with the harvest, hold a lamb, shear a sheep. He had announced proudly that he wanted to be a farmer. His father had guffawed so loudly that Liam had cried. He remembered his mother giving a rare chastising to his father. Douglas Leighton had cut her off quickly and said "No son of mine will be a farmer. Not after the reputation I have built for this family." He had reached across the carriage and ruffled little Liam's strawberry blonde hair. "Perhaps one day, son, you'll have a country house. A summer house. You can have sheep there if you'd like, and when you're a man, you'll have shepherds to care for them. But for now, you'll stay in Montreal. A real man's work lies in Montreal."

CHAPTER TWENTY-EIGHT

Liam rode Babudor down the cobblestone streets. Children grasped their mother's hands and looked up at him in awe. Liam would always catch each child's eye and give him or her a smile.

Riding on slowly past the garment factories, he sighed. What was he really doing with his life? Nothing happened on these shifts; on an exciting day, he'd break up a bar fight between a couple of louts who decided to drink at noon. But what was he really doing? It seemed to Liam that he was putting on a costume and play-acting a person of power.

A pull on his pantleg startled Liam out of his reverie. "Mister!" the small boy said. "There's a fight in the street!"

"Where?" said Liam, immediately at attention.

"The Mercier Factory!" The boy pointed down the south street. "A man just pushed a lady in the street!"

Liam nodded crisply and spurred his horse.

He heard the shouting first.

"You wench, how dare you threaten me?" A barrel of a man stood over a woman who was gripping a bundle and struggling to rise from the curb. The man's jowls shook as the color rose in his face. "I'll pay you what we agreed and not a penny more." He reached a hairy arm down and yanked the woman up. "In fact, I think I'll take these pieces for free," he hissed in her face. "For the trouble you've given me."

Liam reined in the horse. "Stop, immediately," he said, his deep voice ringing into the street.

Mr. Porcher wrinkled his nose and released Anya's arm. He pointed a greasy finger at Liam. "This woman is trying to steal from me. I have a right to run my business. I have a right to my product."

"You have no right to shout at someone in the open street," Liam said, placing his hand on the hilt of his ceremonial sword for emphasis. "You have no right to assault anyone."

"Assault?" yelled Mr. Porcher "This wench assaulted my pride! I am just claiming what was mine."

"Shut your mouth," Liam said. "This woman has every right to be safe in our streets, to go about her business. Are you hurt, Miss?" Liam turned to Anya for the first time.

"No," she said, jutting her proud chin into the air.

Liam swallowed hard. Those eyes, that golden skin. This was the girl from the pier.

"Now will you uphold the law or not?" Mr. Porcher said, wiping his brow. "Those linen pieces belong to me!" He reached forward to rip the bundle out of Anya's arms and she lurched back, causing him to trip and splash himself in muddy slush. Liam leapt off his horse and threw the reins to one of the people gathered near. Turning red in the face, Mr. Porcher roared and grasped at the pearls around Anya's neck. She reached her arm back and slapped him hard across the face. At the same time, Liam grabbed the man's arms and held them fast behind his back.

"You're coming in, sir," Liam said firmly. "Spending a night or two at the pleasure of the Queen."

"The bitch struck me!"

Liam yanked his arms hard. "Shut your mouth. The lady defended herself." Turning to Anya, he asked, "Are you alright, Miss?"

Anya held the bundle close to her chest and threw her shoulders back. "I'm fine." Liam wanted to look closer to see if she had any injuries, but the foreman was wriggling in his grasp. Liam gave him a rough shake for good measure and then said calmly to Anya, "Please come to the Stationhouse. We'll need you to give your statement to press charges."

CHAPTER TWENTY-NINE

Anya pulled her shawl tightly around her shoulders and adjusted her pearls. She didn't meet the eyes of anyone else sitting in the Stationhouse. It was unthinkable that anyone might assume she was there as a criminal. It was almost worse that they know that she had been assaulted in the street.

Officer Leighton had been insistent on speaking to her before she left. She glanced at her small wristwatch. It was teatime and she hadn't eaten since breakfast. If he didn't return within a quarter of an hour, she would walk herself home.

"Sorry for making you wait," a deep voice called from across the room. Liam held up his hand in greeting and then stopped at the desk before making his way to Anya. He rested his elbow on the desk and leaned in to have a few quiet words with the man at the desk. Nodding at the man's words, Liam Leighton reached out and shook his hand. Striding confidently over to Anya, he gave a wide smile. "Miss," he said "Howard says our man is booked up for several nights. He won't be bothering you." Anya stood up, smoothing her dress. She reached for her bundle of embroidered linen and Liam held out his hand. "Please. Allow me."

Anya looked up at him. "Thank you for all you've done, really, Officer, but I must make my way back home now."

"Oh, you shouldn't walk back by yourself after the day you've had," Liam said, offering his arm. "I mean to walk you home." He smiled at her. "If that's alright with you, of course."

Anya hesitated. "Aren't you on duty?"

"Keeping our good citizens safe from ruffians is my duty," he said, his eyes twinkling. "As you said, it's past teatime and dark will be settling in. Please. Allow me to walk you home."

Anya gave him a long look. It felt strange, not having the pinprick of fear or caution that she always seemed to have with men. Even with Cillian, that wave of danger was there, but the excitement of it all had outweighed the terror. With this man, she simply felt free. Safe. She chastised herself for her silliness, but this officer was right about one thing: it was getting dark.

"Fine," she said, and slipped her small hand in the crook of his arm.

CHAPTER THIRTY

When Anya and Liam reached the Leon Street, she slipped her hand from his arm and pointed at a Victorian house with dark maroon bricks. "That's me," she said. Liam let out a low whistle.

"Beautiful," he said. "Your family's home?"

Anya smiled. She thought to the shimmer and sparkle of the granite stones that made the incredible stone house on the island. That was more beautiful than this house could ever be.

"It's a boarding house," she said. "I have a furnished room." She could feel eyes on her from inside the window. What would they say? A tall, young, handsome Mountie walking her home? She'd never hear the end of it; she may have to skip supper.

"Listen, Miss Lyon," Liam was saying. "I would have liked to take you to tea today, especially since you've had such a harrowing experience. But we're not allowed to engage in social activities while in uniform." Liam stole a glance behind her shoulder and saw the curtains peeled back. He looked back at Anya and threw her a wink. "My day off is next Friday. May I take you to tea on Friday?"

Anya looked up at him. Why not? she thought.

"I will see you on Friday," she said, nodding crisply. She tried to sound brusque, but couldn't contain the smile that spread into her eyes.

CHAPTER THIRTY-ONE

Anya smoothed the silk of her plum-colored skirt as she sat nervously in the parlour. Earlier in the day, she had sat, looking out of her window to the east, as was her practice. She closed her eyes and breathed deeply. She concentrated on Officer Leighton's face and tried to discern the Truth. Was he honest? Was he safe?

She used to do this when she thought of Cillian and she shuddered to remember the imaged that had flashed behind her closed eyes. Snakes crawled, gold shimmered in the clouds, so many countless stairs leading up, up, up. She would always come out of these sessions breathless. Much like how she left her meetings with Cillian... A blush rose her to her cheek.

Well. Every day that week, she had tried to remember what she could see of Officer Leighton's face. Perhaps if she had her Spirit Stone to hold in the palm of her hand, she would be able to see more. As it was, she only saw water. Waves. Rocks. Large expanses of land. A forest filled with trees she didn't understand. Nothing otherworldly. Nothing that made her heart race, that stole her breath, that sent fire through her veins. Anya shook her head. Maybe the magic didn't work here in Montreal. Maybe she didn't.

A knock at the door brought her into the present moment. Quickly, she checked her handbag and patted her pocket to ensure she had one of the embroidered handkerchiefs. She stood and straightened the double strand of pearls in the mirror, taking a moment to pat a few stray tendrils of hair back into place. There was no need to pinch her cheeks this afternoon; her color was already high.

Liam entered the front hall at the invitation of Mrs. Carre and Anya tucked herself behind the doorframe, peeking out to take a glance of him. As he doffed his hat, Anya saw his wavy strawberry blonde hair for the first time. Even in the dim light of the hall, it shimmered. Liam had a small posy in his hand, to Anya's surprise, he offered it to Mrs. Carre. Her vinegary cheeks melted into a smile as she accepted the violets.

"Miss Lyon," she called up the stairs. "You have a caller!" Anya cleared her throat and emerged from the parlour.

"Oh," said Mrs. Carre, narrowing her eyes and appraising Anya carefully. "You might've let me know you were downstairs; I wouldn't have raised my voice."

"Sorry," said Anya.

"Go along," said Mrs. Carre, stepping out of the way so Anya could walk through. "And you know the rules: back before dusk. This is a respectable house of respectable people, Officer Leighton.

Liam made his face very serious. "I could tell as soon as I stepped through the door that you are an upstanding citizen. This is clearly a house with the highest reputation. I'll be sure Miss Lyon is back well before the sun sets."

"Very well, very well," Mrs. Carre said, blushing under Liam's gaze. "Have a lovely afternoon." Anya nodded politely to Mrs. Carre and walked through the door that Liam held open for her.

CHAPTER THIRTY-TWO

The street was crowded as people began to return home from work. Liam offered his arm and Anya took it, as much for safety as anything else. Someone as tall as this man would cut through crowds with or without a Mountie uniform.

Liam cleared his throat. "Thank you for agreeing to allow me to take you to tea."

Automatically, Anya said, "It was my pleasure. Thank you."

"You see," Liam interrupted, "I have something for you."

Anya stopped, pulling Liam to a stop as well. She extracted her hand from his arm. "I cannot accept gifts from a man I just met," she said, stepping back.

"Oh, no, it's not a gift," Liam said. "I... I have something that belongs to you." Anya took a second step backward, gauging how quickly it would take for her to run back to the boarding house. Liam caught her expression and breathed out in exasperation at his own awkwardness. "I'm sorry, Miss Lyon, I'm making a mess of this. Please."

Liam gently moved Anya out of the way of the muddy street. "Please let's go to tea. It's just around the corner. I'm muddling this, I'm sorry. It's easier if I explain there."

Anya took a deep breath. How could she get into trouble with a Mountie? In any case, it was a very crowded street. She decided to follow him. What of hers could he possibly have? Everything she didn't leave behind in the village was either on her back or locked safely in her room.

Liam was not lying; the teashop was right around the next corner, tucked into a cornflower blue building with a view of the sea. He asked the maître'd for a table in the window, smiling in that way Anya already recognized. The way that made people happy, that made people want to make him happy. There was nothing false in his smile. As the maître'd led them to their table, Anya found that the tension she had been holding released from her shoulders.

Once seated, Liam politely asked for Anya's opinion on which tea to order. While he immediately agreed, he asked her why she chose the tea she chose. Anya had never been asked something like that before, much less been asked to make the decision in the first place. She wrinkled her nose and gave the briefest of explanations, but he kept peppering her with questions. Before she knew it, she was explaining the particular uses of all the herbs in the blend. Liam leaned his arms on the table, listening intently. As she poured the tea, she half-expected him to mock the taste, or pretend to be dramatically affected by the herbs therein. Instead, he simply said, "Hmm. You're right. This is refreshing. Now," Liam set his tea cup on the saucer. "What should we order to eat? What do you like?"

Anya had been taught to be solicitous and she didn't have much experience in restaurants. But somehow, she found herself saying "I don't care for meat, but I enjoy fish. And sweets. Dark chocolate in particular."

Liam nodded and waved to the server. "Smoked salmon sandwiches please. And cucumber, do you like cucumber? I do." Anya nodded, smiling. "And the profiteroles. Dark chocolate," he said, nodding at her.

"What do you like, Officer Leighton?" Anya asked, reaching out and almost putting her hand on his wrist. She pulled it away just in time. He smiled at her as if he hadn't noticed her forward gesture. "I don't know. Something with cinnamon, perhaps? Cinnamon and lemon."

Anya laughed. "Cinnamon and lemon? That is an interesting combination."

"Well, I'm an interesting person," Liam said, grinning at her. "At least I try to be." He looked up at the server. "Well sir, what do you have with cinnamon and lemon?"

The server held his pen poised over the pad of paper and suppressed an eyeroll. "May I recommend the lemon tart and perhaps the cinnamon roll cake," he said dryly.

Anya scrunched up her face and suppressed her own eyeroll. Liam looked at her for approval. "What do you think?" he asked.

"I think you should order something quickly," Anya said, laughing. "We'll figure it out when it gets here."

"Both then," said Liam, clapping a hand on the table. "Well, all three. The dark chocolate, the lemon tart and the cinnamon bread. Please."

"Right away," the server said, turning on his heel and marching away.

Liam took a deep breath and grinned. "I'm having a nice time," he said, looking at her. "Are you?"

Anya nodded and a smile spread across her face, making her dark brown eyes shine. He held her gaze and the clatter and din of the tearoom seemed to fade away. Any felt a warmth run through her.

"Oh!" Liam patted the pocket of his jacket. "I almost forgot. I have something for you. I can't believe it was you the other day – I can't believe I found you." Reaching in his jacket, he produced a box tied with a bright blue ribbon. Liam saw her look at the ribbon. He looked down and said quickly "I noticed your dress was blue. And I noticed you looking at the sea. I figured you must like blue, so I bought a blue ribbon."

"The sea?" Anya asked.

"When we first met. At the pier." Anya looked at him as if he'd gone mad. Liam pushed the box toward her.

"It's no surprise," he said. "It belongs to you."

Anya took the box in her hand. The weight felt familiar. She carefully untied the ribbon and opened the lid. When she saw what was inside, tears sprung to her eyes. "Where did you find this?"

"You dropped it," Liam said. "When you were at the pier. I think I surprised you."

Anya ran her fingers over the jasper pendant. It held a coolness, like the memories of a lake far away and long ago.

She raised her eyes to Liam. "You do surprise me."

The server arrived with the tea tray. Anya pulled the box toward her and placed it on her side of the table, covering it with her left hand. Liam quickly served each of them and reached across the table to pour more tea. He waited a beat for Anya to eat, but she didn't touch her food. "Does it not look good?" Liam asked.

Leaving her hand over the necklace, Anya reached over and took a small bite of her sandwich. Crumbs spilled on her dress and she looked mortified. Liam smiled at her.

"What, do you think I'm going to reach across the table and steal the necklace back?"

"It's just," Anya started and then looked in his eyes. He looked so sincere; there was nothing hiding there. The clear blue depth of his eyes made her catch her breath. She let out a small sigh and let go of the box, picking up her napkin from her lap to brush the crumbs away. "The necklace is... very special to me."

"Clearly," said Liam. "It's very pretty. Although I don't know what kind of stone it is."

Anya looked at it. The golden veins stretching through the stone seemed to glow. "It's jasper."

"Jasper. Huh. Never heard of that gemstone" Liam reached for another bite and then stopped, aware that she wasn't eating yet.

"It's not a gemstone, it's a..." She almost said 'sacred stone.' But she couldn't possibly tell this man about the Stone Society, here in this tearoom. "It's a lake stone." Her expression turned hard as she remembered Cillian. "It's not valuable."

"That silver work is incredible though," Liam said. "I don't know jewelry, but I know when work is done with skill." Anya found her herself blushing. Gesturing to the necklace, Liam asked, "Why don't you put it on? You'd feel better about letting it go and having a bite to eat, I bet. And I'd like to see it on you."

Anya reached up and touched her pearls. "I'm wearing a necklace already."

"So what?" Liam said, winking at her. "Let's see."

Lifting the necklace out of the box, she was struck with the care he had clearly taken with the chain and the settling of the stone into the velvet cushion. She reached her arms up over her head and fastened the clasp. Arranging it so the delicate chain rested beneath the pearls, she settled the jasper pendant just below her collarbone.

Liam was staring. "Whoa," he said. "That really is beautiful. I've never seen a stone that glows so much."

An older woman sitting near them coughed pointedly. Liam raised his eyes and drew in a quick, embarrassed breath. "Please," he said, gesturing to the food. "Eat."

Anya took a sip of tea and obligingly took a few bites of the food Liam had placed on her plate.

"Do you like it?" he asked.

"This salmon is delicious," she said. "Thank you." She daubed her lips with the napkin and looked up at him. "How did you catch that fisherman?" she asked.

"I'm sorry?"

"The fisherman who stole my necklace," Anya said. "I didn't see you on the dock that day. I mean, I was distracted, but surely I think I would have remembered seeing a Canadian Mountie going after a fisherman-turned thief."

Liam looked at her like she had lost her senses.

"Were you off duty?" Anya asked, reaching up to touch the pendant. "Out of uniform?"

"When I caught your pendant?" Liam asked.

"When you caught the thief." Anya said.

"Thief?" Liam muttered. He scratched his head for a moment and then suddenly burst into laughter. People at the neighboring tables glanced over. Bowing from the neck dramatically, Liam looked at Anya. "The thief was none other than yours truly," he said, still laughing.

"I beg your pardon?" Anya asked.

"I fish. Well, I catch lobster. On the days I'm not on duty. It was me who caught your necklace. You just ran away before I had the chance to tie up my skiff and come up on the pier to give it back to you."

Anya went white. "That was you?" she asked, the color draining from her face.

"That was me," Liam said, placing another salmon sandwich on her plate.

"Then you must have…"

"I was listening to you sing," Liam said. "I could hear you from a little ways out. You have a beautiful voice."

Now the color flushed deeply back into Anya's cheeks. "I thought I was alone," she said.

"Please don't be embarrassed," Liam said. "Truly, your song drew me in. I felt like I might be intruding but I really couldn't help it. I mean, I play the fiddle a little bit, but nothing like that. Music like that… well… That comes from a place deep inside."

"Well," Anya said, and then stopped, looking down at the napkin in her lap. When she forced herself to raise her eyes, Liam held her gaze. She assessed this man who was sitting in front of her. Listening.

The server placed the bill in front of Liam with a clearing of his throat. "Sir. Miss. We will be closing soon. The supper hour approaches."

"Of course." Liam held up his hand for the man to wait and withdrew several bills from his pocket. The server took them and stepped away. "Miss Lyon," Liam said, turning to Anya. "I'd like to see you again. Would you like to see me again?"

The jasper brooch began to feel warm against Anya's skin. Who was this man, this tall, thin man with the wide-set blue eyes and bowed lips. After Cillian, Anya promised herself that she would not trust any man, would not let down the barriers she built around her heart. She would study and work and perfect her skills and somehow, find a way. Find a path. Make meaning of her life.

"Do you know," Anya said, smiling across the table at Liam. "I believe I would."

CHAPTER THIRTY-THREE

Candlelight made the dark wood of the pub glow even as pipe smoke curled in the air. The room seemed to vibrate with the sound of music and laughter.

The hall was crowded. The sound of laughter and clinking glasses made Anya take a deep breath in. The jasper pendant hung just below her collarbone, touching the lace neckline of her lavender gown. Liam took her hand without thinking twice and led her through the crowd. Being a head taller than most of them, it was easy to get through. They approached a table and the gentleman stood up, a head shorter than Liam. He reached out a muscular arm and shook Liam's hand. The shorter man pulled Liam closer and clapped him on the back. Liam grinned down at Anya and said, "This is Caleb."

Caleb grinned at Anya. "So you are the famous Miss Lyon," he said. He held his hand out. Anya took it and Caleb placed a second warm hand on hers, smiling gently. "Liam talks of nothing else."

Anya stole a look at Liam and turned to Caleb. "Please, call me Anya."

"Anya," Caleb said, releasing her hand and offering his arm to the pretty blonde sitting at the table. "This is Madeline," he said, beaming. "My fiancée."

Madeline smiled. "Lovely to meet you, Anya," she said. "Glad someone can finally put up with our Liam."

Liam rolled his eyes and leaned down to give Madeline a hug. "Let's get some pints, what do you say?" Liam clapped Caleb on the back and turned to Anya. "A pint alright for you?" Anya thought of the hot, fiery whiskey she used to drink on the island with her Aunt before sessions. She hadn't had a drink since arriving in Quebec, but what would be the harm in a pint of ale?

"Alright," she said.

Liam leaned down and whispered, "A pint, and then a dance," he said. "Promise?" Anya couldn't suppress a grin as she watched men walked toward the bar. Madeline sat, arranging her skirts.

"May I?" asked Anya.

"Of course!" Madeline said, gesturing to the chair opposite.

"Congratulations on your wedding," Anya said politely. "Caleb seems like a lovely man. When do you get married?"

"In just about a month," Madeline said, placing a protective hand her belly. "And it couldn't come soon enough. Caleb and I have been sweethearts since we left school." Anya thought of Cillian and Hannah. Hannah must have had his baby by now. Color drained from her cheeks. Madeline saw Anya's expression folded her hands together. "I'm sorry," she said, "I don't mean to shock you."

"Oh, I'm not shocked," Anya said, attempting to arrange her mouth into a smile. "Where there's love… well, the more people you can love, the better off you are." she said.

Madeline smiled at her and suddenly reached out to squeeze her hand. "You're sweet," she said. "I have a sense we'll be great friends. Liam adores you, you know."

"I've only met him twice," Anya said, laughing. "Well, three times, I suppose, but I didn't know who he was the first time…"

"Well, twice is enough for Liam. He said –"

"Ladies!" Caleb stepped forward and set two pints of amber ale down. "You must be parched with all of that talking. Take a sip and then let's take a spin."

Liam watched intently as Anya took a small sip of her drink. His eyebrows furrowed. "It's too strong for you, isn't it?" he asked.

Anya threw her head back and let out a hearty laugh. "I'm much stronger than this," she said. Raising her glass to Liam and his friends, she downed the pint. Liam said nothing, only raised his eyebrows with pride and reached out his hand. "Well," he said, "We know you can drink, let's see if you can jig."

Anya set her glass down and put her small hand in his large thin one.

The music flew through the air and the beat pulsed as the bodhran player hit the skin of his drum with the beater. Anya hitched her skirt in one hand and placed her hand on Liam's shoulder. She felt his warm, large palm at the small of her back and they began to spin around the room. The song changed key and became higher and brighter. Liam took her left hand and placed it around his neck. Anya blushed as she felt the soft strands of his hair brush her fingertips.

"Mason's Apron," Liam said, twirling them past another couple.

"What?" Anya asked.

"The song," Liam said, smiling. "It's called Mason's Apron."

"You know this song?" Anya asked.

"I know all of these songs," Liam said. "I play the fiddle. Have done since I was a boy."

"Well," Anya said, trying to make her feet keep time with the fast tempo of the song. "I'd like to hear that."

"Would you?" Liam asked, a twinkle glinting in his eye. "Well, I'll make you a deal, Miss Lyon."

"Anya."

Liam slowed their steps to half time. "Anya?" he asked.

"Anya," she said, holding his gaze.

Liam grinned. "Well, Anya," he said, "My deal is this. You have the most beautiful voice I've ever heard. I'll play for you, if you sing for me."

Anya rolled her eyes and laughed. "Deal," she said. "Liam."

"Liam." He nodded, trying to keep his smile calm. "I like that."

The song changed. The tune seemed strained and wailing and Anya couldn't suppress the look on her face. Liam sucked in his breath. "This one is called 'Bagpipe on a Violin," he said, grimacing. "Let's take a break."

He led Anya back to the table and they chatted, watching the other dancers for a few more songs. Caleb and Madeline were dancing slowly and Liam waved his hand in greeting. Both waved back.

"Would you like another pint?" Liam asked.

"No thank you. I did drink the last one a bit quickly," Anya said.

"Yes you did!" Liam reached across the table and covered her hand with his. "You're such an interesting girl," he said.

Now it was her turn to grimace. "Interesting," she said. "I'm not sure that's the compliment I was hoping for."

"Well, you know you're beautiful," Liam said, leaning back and crossing his arms in mock assessment. "You must know that. And you know you're smart. You have to be a smart person to be able to live alone in a city like this. And you're talented, making that embroidery,

138

and the singing. But you are interesting. What's wrong with interesting?"

Anya burst into laughter. Who was this man who was so honest, who held no trace of mystery, who held nothing back? Who spoke like this?

Liam put his hand to his chest with mock offense. "Are you laughing at me, Miss Lyon?" he said. "I am an officer of the Royal Canadian Mounted Police! I am a very serious person."

"Yes, I am well aware," Anya said, biting her lip to try to control the stream of laughter. She looked at him, at those glowing blue eyes, and suddenly the memory of the man in the factory screaming at her, trying to throw her in the street flooded back. The smile melted from her face and she looked at him.

"Liam, I wanted to thank you for..." She swallowed hard. "For stopping that awful man that day outside the factory –"

Liam held up his hand.

"That man was a scoundrel. He doesn't belong around decent people and he certainly doesn't belong in our fun here tonight."

"But-" Anya started

"You can't thank me for doing my job. That's my job, to keep scoundrels like that off the streets. It's why I joined the mounted police. And that day, I was doing my job."

"Well, you can't tell me what to do, Officer Leighton," Anya said with an arch of her eyebrows. "I will thank you if I want to. So, thank you."

Liam looked at her for a moment, grinning. He threw up his hands in mock surrender. "You are welcome, Miss Lyon," he said. "Now, this is 'Bird in a Tree,'" he said. "Let's dance."

Liam and Anya danced to several more tunes, grinning and talking. Occasionally they stopped and joined Madeline and Caleb at the table for refreshments. Soon, Anya and Madeline were chatting like old friends, Anya offering some advice for teas and herbs that would help Madeline in the months to come.

The ladies were head to head chatting when a gentleman came to the table and tapped Liam on the shoulder. He leaned in and the men spoke in quiet tones. Caleb looked over and listened, then began to smile.

"Go on," said Caleb. "I'll take care of the ladies."

Anya looked at Liam questioningly. He winked at her and strode off without a word. Anya looked at Caleb who asked, "Can I get you anything, Anya?" She shook her head and smiled at him. Anya tried to see where Liam had gone, but he was already swallowed up by the crowd. Anya sighed, taking a sip of her ale.

A new tune started at the front of the room, a fast melody that began with a long, low pull on a fiddle followed by a cluster of faster, climbing notes. Anya recognized the song, had heard it a thousand times at home. A smile burst across her face and she looked for

Liam, straining to see him in the crowded room. She found herself hoping he would return before the end of the song.

She would ask him to dance.

"Oh, there he goes!" said Caleb, beginning to clap and stomp to the beat. Madeline grinned and turned to Anya. "He is good, isn't he?" she asked.

"Who?" Anya around.

"Liam!" Madeline said. "Look there!" She pointed at the stage. At the center, taller than any of the musicians, stood Liam, grinning and sawing away on a fiddle.

"How..." stammered Anya. "He didn't even bring an instrument."

"Oh, he always finds a way to get what he needs," Caleb said. "I'm sure he borrowed one."

As the tune flew through the air, tears began to well up in Anya's eyes.

"Oh, Anya, I hope you're not upset!" Madeline said, offering her handkerchief. "I'm sure he's only trying to impress you." Anya waved her away and put her fingertips up to her eyelids to catch the tears before they fell.

"I'm not upset at all," she said. "Just a bit homesick." She coughed lightly, gaining control of her tears. "The song they're playing is from my... where I grew up. It's called St. John's Reel."

"You grew up in St. John's?" Madeline said. "One hears stories about that haunted island off of the mainland. Have you heard of that place?"

"That is a tale," Anya said, a bit more harshly than she meant.

As the song ended, Anya swallowed hard and looked up at the stage. Liam was beaming at her. The drummer stood and applauded Liam. "Liam Leighton, everyone! Our resident brave Mountie turned fiddle player extraordinaire!" Liam lowered his head under the roaring applause. After a moment, he waved the applause away. "Stop, please," he shouted. "You know I love playing for you all, but tonight there is a musician in the house who is better than I could ever be."

Instinctively, Anya looked around for Cillian and her heart seized.

"Anya, he's calling to you." Anya turned to Caleb in alarm. "Go on!" Caleb was saying. Anya glanced up and realized the entire pub was looking at her expectantly.

"Straight from St. John's," Liam was shouting from the stage. "The most beautiful voice you will ever hear. Come on up, Miss Lyon!" Anya stared at him, unbelieving. Caleb slid a nearly-full pint glass across the table.

"Take some liquid courage," he said softly. "And don't worry – everyone in here has had more than enough liquid courage."

Anya looked from the left to the right. Some faces were smiling, some beckoning, some looked skeptical. In her mind, she had two choices – run out of the pub and back to the boarding house and never see these people again, or go up there and sing a song. She knew none of them, she would never have to see any of them again if she didn't want to, including that blasted Liam. What did it matter what they thought of her? The image of Hannah with her hand on her belly jumped in front of her memory. Anya gripped the pint glass tightly. She looked at Liam, who had begun to look rather sheepish. The tension in the room was palatable. Anya took a breath and stood up. Raising her glass in salute to the stage, she downed the rest of the ale and walked onto the stage amidst a roar of applause.

CHAPTER THIRTY-FOUR

Liam extended his hand to help her onto the stage. He grinned at her and leaned over.

"You're good," he whispered in her ear. "Better than any of these fools." He gave her hand a quick kiss. The room erupted in applause. "Better than me by far," he said, leading her toward the front of the stage.

"Miss Anya Lyon!" Liam spread his hands wide as he shouted to the room and turned to face her, joining the raucous applause. "Now," he said, turning to Anya and the rest of the musicians. "What are we playing?"

"This was your idea," said Anya. "I have no idea what you all know."

Liam waved her query away. "They can play anything. They'll figure it out. What do you want to sing?"

A catalogue of songs ran through Anya's head, all the old Scots-Gaelic ones she knew were slow, and might disturb the raucous mood of the pub. Cillian's harp tunes she could sing, but the very thought of it stabbed at her heart.

Liam saw the expression on her face and leaned forward. "I really didn't mean for you to be this worried, Anya. I'm sorry."

Anya clenched her teeth and looked away. Forcing Cillian and his songs out of her mind, she pulled her shoulders back. She thought of the songs she used to hear her father sing when he'd had a few glasses of beer. She turned around to the rest of the musicians. "Do you know 'Down by the Bonny Glen?'" she asked.

Smiling and nodding to her, they raised their instruments.

"Will you sing the first few bars to me, Anya, so we can get the key?" Liam asked

Anya sang quietly in his ear and Liam played a few accompanying notes on his fiddle. Nodding, he turned over his shoulder. "Key of E-flat," he said. "Not too fast."

Holding the fiddle on his shoulder with his chin, he gestured to her with the bow.

Anya began to sing, the notes flowing through her. Her voice was warm and full and bright, and she floated through the phrases. Liam followed her exactly, grinning as he stroked the strings with his bow, crescendoing when she got louder, drawing his instrument back as she dimenuendoed. At the ends of each phrase, Liam would be sure to play softer than she sang, so her natural vibrato would shine through the room.

People were grinning and soon began to clap along. When the song was over, Liam reached over and threw an arm around her waist, kissing her cheek. "Beautiful!" he said. "You put the wind into everyone's sails. It was fun, wasn't it?"

Anya couldn't help grinning back. She leaned into his embrace. "It was fun," she said, looking into his bright blue eyes.

"Well then, let's play another!" She rolled her eyes at him and turned to thank the rest of the musicians. They were all looking at her admirably, agreeing heartily with Liam that of course they should all play more. "Whatever you know, we'll play," the bodhran player said.

Anya took a deep breath and looked at the room. "Another!" shouted a man at the back. His cry was echoed by several patrons. "Come on lassie, give us a song!" another patron called. Liam shrugged and opened his hands.

"It doesn't seem like you have a choice," he said.

"I always have a choice," retorted Anya. She turned to the musicians. "'The Bay of Lochmore', shall we?" She turned to the room and let out the first, clear, high note. On cue, the musicians flew to accompany her.

Liam, Anya, and the rest of the band performed every up-tempo song she could remember and some she did not. Liam taught her the songs and she followed along, grinning and laughing as she tried to anticipate his lyrics. The room ate it up, and people danced and laughed and raised their glasses until finally, the barkeep stepped onto the stage.

"Ladies and gentlemen," he shouted over the crowd. "Ladies and gentlemen please!" He spread his arms as if to quiet the crowd, who groaned and booed. The barkeep grinned. "I know, I know. She's brighter than the stars in the sky. But the sun will rise soon and we must close. It is the law, after all." The booing got louder and Liam stepped forward and said a word in the barkeep's ear. The man raised one eyebrow and looked at Anya.

"Ask her," Liam said.

The owner stepped to Anya. "Young lady," he said. "Your man Liam says that you would like to sing some slower tunes. Perhaps calm the room down."

Anya shook her head. "I never said that," she said, brushing her hands on her skirt.

"Come on now, go ahead," said Liam. "Sing what you sang on the pier that day." Turning to the barkeep, Liam said "Promise them one more song out of us. If she sings one more for them, they have to leave. A compromise." Liam turned to Anya. "Would you?" he asked?

Anya took a deep breath. The people in the room had had so much ale, it wouldn't matter whether they understood her song or not. They wouldn't know the magic in it, wouldn't feel the meaning. And so, it was not as terrifying to sing. Not as private. She turned to the barkeep.

"We can give them one more."

The barkeep nodded and turned to the crowd. "Now will ye shut the feck up?" he said with a smile. "The lady has agreed to one more song. If – providing that's an if – you lot promise to clear out after she'd finished."

A cheer erupted in the room and people stood, expecting one more raucous dance.

Anya closed her eyes and took a breath. When she exhaled, it seemed like a gentle wind blew through the room. Anya began the low, lilting first notes of Uisdeen Fireen. She closed her eyes as she sang the first verse, remembering the light in her mother's eyes as she sang to Anya in her cradle, in the kitchen, when she taught her to sew, to embroider. Anya allowed herself to remember the last time she had sung this tune, at her mother's bedside on those last, snow-buried days.

From far off and yet within her heart, a keening harmony brought her to the present. A bow stroked across strings, adding depth to her melody. Anya's eyes fluttered open and she saw Liam, standing next to her, finding a way into the song she sang. They played together for a verse and chorus, and eventually the rest of the players wove their music around Anya's melody. Using her breath, Anya pulled them through the aching of the rising lines. She floated above the descents, making space for the falling, hanging each lowered note by a tense string. The musicians followed her, finding the intensity of Anya's heart, holding onto the beauty they

148

created, controlling each note until finally, together, they burst into a crescendo. A chord hung above the crowd, making the very air tremble.

The final note of the song rode in Anya's voice and floated above the room. When it had fluttered away, the room was completely silent. The people who had been standing to dance remained standing, jaws hanging loose. Mouths open. Some wiped tears from their eyes as they were released from the spell of the song.

Anya looked around the room and saw people seemingly in a state of shock begin to reach for anything, a pint glass, a handbag, the living, breathing skin of the person beside them, trying to find an anchor back into reality.

Finally, after several moments, applause guttered through the room, building into an eruption of cheers and hollers. Anya looked back to Liam.

His face held every emotion she might name. No one had looked at her like that before. She stepped back toward him and he shook his head. With one hand holding his fiddle, he gestured with the other for her to step into the light.

CHAPTER THIRTY-FIVE

Liam held Anya hand as if he would never let it go. They walked together, neither saying much, Anya turning her face to the east to feel the warmth of the first rays of sunshine.

Liam led them over to the beginning of the pier and they rested tired elbows on the railing.

"What do you see?" asked Liam.

"I'm not sure," Anya said to the sea. Anya looked up at him and saw nothing in his eyes that was not goodness. She rested her head on his hard, thin arm, not quite tall enough to reach his shoulder. He swallowed hard. Anya felt his gentle kiss in her hair.

"I should go home," she said.

"You are home," Liam whispered. His voice was so soft that he thought she may not have heard him. The sweet pressure of her kiss on his jacket sleeve told him that she did.

They stayed, leaning into each other, watching the rose-colored sun spill onto the horizon. The star-shimmering silver arc above the sun transformed into a gold that washed the night sky clean of her mystery.

The rough call of the stevedores startled Liam, and he wrapped an arm protectively around Anya. Her mahogany hair had fallen well and truly out of its careful chignon, and rested in waves around her collarbone. The wind gently played with the loose strands around her face. Liam looked down at her and watched as she absently brushed a strand of hair out of her eyes. Those dark, indigo eyes that held his gaze as she sang, those eyes that looked now out to the sea as if she knew its secrets.

Wind gusted up and Anya nuzzled against Liam's coat and yawned. The sound of the stevedores was getting closer and Liam could hear the men as they began to stomp up and down the docks. He kissed Anya's hair again and reached across her waist to squeeze her hand. "We should get you home," he said. Anya looked up at him, mesmerized by the clear blue of his eyes. How were they the color of the new spring moss one minute, and the color of the sky the next?

They walked to Anya's boarding house hand in hand. It seemed to Liam as if he was walking on a cloud; no spot of mud could mar his boot, no nighttime stench could offend his nose, not even the cobblestones on the streets could trip his gait if only he were standing next to her.

Anya felt so free, more than she had felt in her entire life. Something had lifted from her, a burden that she didn't know she carried.

"Miss Lyon." A sharp female voice cut through Anya's thoughts. Mrs. Carre stood at the steps of the boarding house, arms crossed, and lips pinched tight. "When your room was empty at dawn, I feared you had been hurt or killed." She gave Liam a long look and raised her eyebrows. "Now I see it has been worse than that." Anya took a step toward the house. Mrs. Carre put her hand out. "We are a respectable boarding house here," she said. "Not a brothel."

"Ma'am please," Liam began but Mrs. Carre advanced down the porch steps.

"I'll have none of your cheek," Mrs. Carre said. "A Canadian Royal Mounted Officer indeed. I expected our men to have more dignity than this, but I suppose I have only myself to blame."

"Mrs. Carre, there has been a great misunderstanding," Anya said, stepping in front of Liam. "We were only out with friends. Officer Leighton walked me home. After what happened in the streets last time –"

"Oh I certainly know about last time!" Mrs. Carre harrumphed. "And now that the sun is shining, I'm beginning to think that that ruckus wasn't the poor Mr. Porcher's fault either. As I say, it must have been my fault to take in a girl with no references, no family."

"I have a family," protested Anya, fury flying through her veins.

152

"Not as I can see," Mrs. Carre. She turned behind her and lifted Anya's carpetbag, holding it out like a dead fish. "You have no family here to keep you on the straight and narrow and as of this morning, my girl, you will not be a resident of this house."

"I'm her family," Liam said suddenly. "I'll be her family." He stepped forward and took Anya's carpetbag, setting it carefully on the bottom step. He turned to Anya and saw in her eyes a whirlpool of fear and fury. He placed a strong warm hand on each of her shoulders. "Marry me, Anya," he said. She looked up at him; no words were able to escape her throat. Grasping her hands in his own, he took a step in closer so that the space between them could fit only the morning air. He leaned down toward her. "Come on, Anya. Let's get married. After tonight, I can't imagine one day with you not in it."

A tear escaped and ran down Anya's cheek. Her hand flew up to brush it away. Liam reached up and daubed the tear with his finger, placing her hand back in his. "Be my wife," he said. "You're the most interesting girl I've ever met, and you're beautiful and talented besides. Let's live a life together, Anya." He leaned forward suddenly and kissed her forehead. "Please."

Anya looked up at him. Those clear, earnest eyes. The long, strong fingers grasping her own, the small shimmer of sweat on his palms. What was she doing? she asked herself. She had run away from Airmed, run away from what she had vowed to learn. Run from the Island, from its rules and she had run from the stricter rules of St. John's. Cillian was lost to her, her father had turned away, had turned his heart to another. She had made it to Montreal, but for what purpose? Almost starving to death, trying to eke out a living embroidering cloth for women who could not appreciate the beauty, could not feel the magic, would just throw her work in the rubbish bin when it got soiled? She lived in a rented room that would never be her home, practicing the old ways alone?

And here was this man with hair the color of gold and eyes that spoke of a clear inland lake. He would not take more than she gave him, he would not tear at her heart only to have the pleasure of mending it. He would not break her. She would not let him.

Liam's grip around her hands grew a little bit tighter and he bit his lower lip.

There was nothing to lose, Anya thought. Only a path forward.

"Yes," she said. She squeezed his hands. "I will marry you, Liam Leighton."

He burst into a grin and before he could say a word, she stood up on her tiptoes and brought her lips to his.

Liam's world felt as if it was cracking underneath his feet. He wrapped his arms around Anya and kissed her deeply. By now, a few onlookers had moved out from behind their curtains and into the street. A few began to hoot and holler. Liam released Anya and stared at her as if he had caught a diamond in his hand. "I can't believe this is happening," he said, beaming. "My wife." He gave Anya one more kiss and turned to Mrs. Carre.

"Now ma'am," he said, still grinning. "I would politely ask that you step aside so that my wife can collect the rest of her things."

Mrs. Carre rolled her eyes and pursed her lip, but moved out of the way of the door. "Just you make sure you get this girl to the church."

Anya gave Liam's hand a quick squeeze and marched past Mrs. Carre and up the stairs, gathering her things as quickly as she could.

CHAPTER THIRTY-SIX

Anya lived with Caleb and Madeline until the wedding, teaching Madeline how to brew herbs to make her pregnancy more comfortable, even teaching her some embroidery techniques. For her part, Madeline introduced Anya to women who would buy and sell embroidery work, and she began to make even more income than she made working for Mr. Porcher. She insisted on giving a portion of what she earned to Caleb and Madeline. For the baby, she said. In the evenings, Liam would join them for dinner, and they would sit around the fireside laughing and talking, Madeline curled up against Caleb's shoulder with an afghan over her growing belly and Anya in a chair working on her wedding dress.

After a few weeks, Liam burst through the door with a grin. "I've got the church," he said, lifting Anya off her feet and planting a kiss on her lips. He set her down and went off to find Caleb. "Sorry, mate," he said. "It looks like I'll be getting married before you!" He clapped Caleb on the shoulder. Caleb rose from the table and embraced him and Madeline did the same, kissing Liam on both cheeks.

Anya followed him to the kitchen. "You've gotten the church?" she asked from the doorway.

"Yes!" Liam said, holding out a piece of paper. "Next Sunday, can you believe it? I hope that wedding dress is ready," he said, pointing a finger at Anya and grinning. Caleb was pouring drams of whiskey for all of them and Madeline had begun to make a bit of refreshment.

"It's not ready by half," Anya said under her breath. Madeline looked over her shoulder at Anya.

"Don't worry, love," she said. "I don't mind that you're getting married first. We've been planning our wedding for a year; the whole family will be there." She laughed and patted her belly. "Maybe that's why I'm in this pickle."

Liam reached down and kissed Madeline on the cheek. "Soon you'll have a friend with you with a baby in her belly." He looked at Anya and color rose to his cheeks. "Right, wife of mine?"

Anya thought of her mother, thought of the color that left her cheeks time after time. She thought of Cillian's accusation, asking why her belly never grew. Mariloup's words at her father's wedding; "a burden on the way – for most women." How could she explain any of this to Liam?

She wasn't ready for a wedding, what was he thinking? Her dress would not be done; she hadn't heard from her father even though she had written twice. And

Aunt Airmed... Anya hadn't even decided whether she would write to her yet. Tears sprang to her eyes.

Liam saw Anya's fallen face and his brows furrowed in consternation. He stepped past Caleb and Madeline and went to the doorway where Anya stood. Taking her hand, he asked, "What is it? What are you afraid of?"

Anya looked up at him. How could she even begin to explain all the things she was afraid of? He brushed a tear away from her cheek and gazed at her, worry written on his face. "It's my father," Anya finally said, swallowing hard. That reason would be the easiest for him to understand. "He hasn't written back yet. I'm sure he can't be here by next Sunday."

Liam took a big breath. He started to say something, and then stopped, gathering Anya into an embrace. "Let me bring your cloak," Liam said. "Let's walk to the pier." Waving away Caleb and Madeline's concerned expressions, Liam quickly gathered Anya's cloak and his overcoat from the hallway. Draping the cloak over her shoulders, he led her outside.

A bracing wind struck them as soon as they stepped off the porch. "I don't have my muff," Anya said, starting to turn.

"Take my hand, then," Liam said, taking one of her small hands in his large one. "Let's walk."

The two of them walked in silence for several blocks, Anya stopping briefly to lift the hood of her cloak over her hair. Liam looked at her and could not see her eyes. He took a deep breath and led them to the edge of the pier.

"I've written to your father, Anya," he said, looking out at the dark water. "Several times, in fact."

Anya turned to look up at him. "You have?"

"Well, I wrote first introducing myself. And asking for his blessing for us to marry."

It felt to Anya like her heart would stop. "What did he say?"

Liam looked at her. "The thing is," he said, "Nothing."

"Nothing?"

"He didn't write back, Anya." Liam gave her hand another squeeze and then tentatively placed his arm around her shoulder. She stood stiffly. "I wrote a few more times. Three. I never received an answer." Liam sighed and gripped the railing of the pier with both hands. "And the letters were never returned either. So he had to have received them."

"Mariloup," Anya said through clenched teeth.

"Who is Mariloup?" Liam asked.

"My father's wife," Anya said, glaring out at the clouds.

"Your mother?"

Anya crossed her arms. "Never," she said. "Mariloup married my father after my mother died trying to give him a son." Anya swallowed hard to keep her composure. Liam looked down at her in pity, but she refused to meet his eyes. "Mariloup swooped in, into my home, into my mother's home. She convinced my father to marry her, and he did and now…" A tear fell and she brushed it away angrily.

"Anya, I'm sorry, I didn't know." Liam stepped toward her and folded her stiff body against his own. She clenched all of her muscles inward. He did not let go. "Do you want to wait until they can come?" he asked.

Anya shook her head almost imperceptibly. "No," she whispered. "There's no point."

"Well," Liam began, but Anya interrupted.

"They've all abandoned me to live their lives," she said. "They've decided I should be on my own. I suppose they have no need for me anymore."

"I can't believe that's true," Liam said.

"You really don't know what the truth is," Anya snapped. She heard him suck in a breath, but his arms stayed tightly around her "…the truth about my family," she continued. "My people."

"I know that I love you," Liam said, placing a hand on the back of her head, nestling her close. "I know that's the truth. And I know you love me. Let me be your family."

Anya swallowed hard. Love. Whatever this was, was it love? She had only known him for a matter of weeks, and besides, how could it be love if there was not some passion and pain? And how could love live where all the truth did not?

Cillian's face flew into her mind's eye. She had loved him. Truth wasn't there either. But love was.

Anya felt Liam's heart beat faster under the cloth of his jacket. Her future was coming, regardless of whether she was ready or not. But there was one way she might see what it held. She raised her eyes to Liam.

"I do love you," she said quietly. "Please, may we go home?"

CHAPTER THIRTY-SEVEN

"Goodnight," he whispered, reaching for her hand to kiss it.

"Goodnight," Anya said, turning to smile at him one last time before she opened the door.

Once inside, Anya put both hands on the door and closed it slowly and silently. Removing her shoes so she wouldn't make a sound, she picked them up and tiptoed into the kitchen. It was imperative that she make some tea. If she chose the herbs carefully, she may be able to divine what she needed to know about Liam. She placed lavender, motherwort, bay leaf, and honeysuckle into the rose-painted teapot.

Once in her room, Anya set the teapot down on the bureau and locked the door. Folding her bedding into a cushion under the open window, she stood and stirred the tea, first counterclockwise. Whispering "May the mundane fade away," she stirred the spoon counterclockwise in the rose-painted teapot. When the tea began to swirl, she lifted the spoon and waited until the liquid came to a standstill. When the water was still, Anya took a deep breath in and exhaled slowly. "May the mundane be gone," she whispered.

She took the spoon and began to stir clockwise. "May the eternal come to me. May the Spirit show me what is to come, and what lay buried." Anya stirred nine times and waited again until the water was still. She leaned over the open teapot and inhaled the scented steam air. Placing the golden-rimmed lid on the teapot, Anya brought forward the simple china teacup she had purchased with her first profits from the embroidery. From the cupboard, she pulled down a small bottle of scotch she had nipped from the cupboard at home before she left. She poured a dram in her teacup, poured the tea over it, and stirred.

Anya brought the teacup over to the window and held it to the moonlight. Next, she lit a candle and set it on the floor in front of the blankets. She brought the flame over the teacup and finally, drank a long sip of the tea. Anya began to breathe deeply. As Airmed had taught her to do, she let the thoughts come and then slowly fade away. She pictured the thoughts of Liam, of Caleb, of the night at the pub, and Cillian's face that slithered into her thoughts whenever she did not guard them. All of these, she pictured falling softly into the depths.

Anya concentrated on Liam's face. She had done this before, after he had taken her to the tea shop. The only thing she saw were waves. Trees. Nothing symbolic, otherworldly. No feeling like she was flying, that beautiful feeling she sometimes reached when she tried to concentrate on her mother.

It was forbidden, she knew, to try to contact those who had died. You could wander too close to the veil, Airmed had said. Too close to the edge. Anya squeezed her eyes tight as she remembered that first excruciating week on the Island after her mother's death, begging Airmed to help her contact her mother, remembering Airmed's harsh rebuke. Surely her mother would keep her safe, Anya argued. Surely her mother would not let her fall into the abyss beyond the veil. What she didn't ask Airmed was, what if she wanted to fall across the veil? It would be easier, Anya thought at times, to be lost forever.

Anya's eyes snapped open and the dark, dusty room opened before her. Silently chastising herself for her lack of concentration, she took another deep drink of the tea. The whiskey warmed her veins and she forced herself to relax her shoulders and open her mind.

Liam. Liam Leighton. She brought to the front of her mind his smile, the feeling of her hand in his. The long, tapered fingers grasping hers, his tall legs flying her across the floor in a dance. She urged the image to turn

163

into something else, breathing deeply. Without opening her eyes, she reached up and unclasped her jasper necklace. Bringing the stone to the palm of her hand, the warmth it held from her skin.

Anya opened her eyes to the jasper. Her vision had become blurrier, but it allowed her to see the pictures in the jasper. This stone had brought her hundreds of pictures, she saw so much. Surely, she could see something, something to be interpreted with Liam. Anything. A bird's wing, a pathway. She brought the stone close to her face.

Nothing.

Nothing except the same tree with roots she had seen before. And waves. And dots, that seemed to grow flicker and grow larger. She sighed. It must be her eyesight, tired from the dim light in the room and the tension of the days.

Anya rested her head against the windowsill. What could possibly be interpreted from a tree? There were trees all around them, there were trees everywhere. If she could discern the type of tree maybe, but… the stone showed her the outline only.

Maybe the sign was that there was no sign. That Liam was ordinary; one in a bunch. Just a man, a normal, ordinary, upstanding man. Nothing special, nothing magical. But maybe that in itself was unique. Or important.

Anya sighed. Maybe she was just not as good at this as she thought. She drained the tea and tried again.

Feeling a buzzing in her head, Anya saw a pathway emerging, one with sharp mountains and pointed archways. Everything was scorching and burnt. The scene glowed with a malicious internal fire. A voice spoke. "You are here. You have brought yourself here. You will see what lies ahead, if you insist." Anya was chilled to the bone, but felt the dry heat from the arched stones around her.

In her mind's eye, Anya walked through an archway and found herself above the sea. Like a bird, she floated above the water. A giant wave rose in her mind's vision. It was enormous, overwhelming, and there was something within it. There was something alive inside the wave, something with a beating heart.

A dark-haired man burst into her vision, his face twisted into a grotesque scream. She saw a mountain yet it wasn't a mountain, it was moving. Powerful and beautiful, it came into the vision. The man disappeared, screaming under the mountain and Liam reached for him, but his arms were frozen stiff.

A slam jolted Anya back into full consciousness. Her eyes flew open and the dark, dusty room revealed itself slowly into her vision. She swallowed hard and tried to catch her breath. Madeline or Caleb must be stirring.

Anya reached over the bed and pulled her shawl from where she had tossed it and draped it across her shoulders. An exhaustion overcame her and her eyes blurred again. Almost without thinking, Anya unbuttoned her dress and pulled it over her head. Loosening the strings of her corset, she stepped out of it and dropped it to the floor. Crawling into bed, she fell into a deep sleep.

CHAPTER THIRTY-EIGHT

The wind rattled the windowpanes. The sound startled Anya awake. She sat up hard in the bed, tangled in the sheets, covered in sweat. Taking a shuddering breath, she gazed around the room. All the detritus of last night's "Seeing" lay scattered about. Including the bottle of whiskey. Anya reached her hand under the nape of her neck to grasp the jasper necklace that had twisted around her neck.

She stepped over the teapot, still lying on the floor. She was drawn like a magnet to the window. The lace curtains fluttered gently, the wind sneaking through to shake them. Anya bit her lip.

The wind, her Aunt Airmed had said. The wind. What was the wind telling her – what was the Seeing telling her? The man in the boat, dark haired and thin, falling under the mountain that moved… who was he?

China clattered downstairs as Madeline began to get breakfast together before Caleb went to work. Anya knew it was late, knew that she should help her friend, but the knot in her stomach froze her.

She pressed her forehead to the cold windowpane and squeezed her eyes shut. The wind screamed and whistled around her. She could not see the face of the man with Liam but she saw his shape. She saw his sinewy arm go under the water, the white fury of the waves as they washed over his dark hair. A ring on his finger, unfamiliar, a woman screaming in the distance. The scream shot into her brain, made her clutch her stomach as if she would be sick, cramping and squeezing as if there was a scream inside her belly as well.

Mariloup.

The woman she could hear in the vision must be Mariloup, that was why her stomach clenched so. She always felt sick around Mariloup, the sight of the woman made her ill. And the ring on the finger – why she didn't recognize it –

Anya's eye snapped open and she gasped. Her father. Her father's hand with his new ring, falling off a ship, falling into the water. Going under, the waves washing over his hair. And Liam- why was Liam there? Why was he reaching for her father?

Anya's breath came quickly as perspiration gathered under her arms. Liam was reaching in the vision because Liam had written to her father trying to get him to come over for the wedding. The screaming was Mariloup trying to prevent it and the falling –

Tears smarted at the corners of her eyes. The Seeing was her father trying to come over on the ship, trying to come to her wedding. The ship would sink! Her father would drown, that was what the vision was telling her. She had to write to him, tell him not to come. But he would come – surely he would come if he got her letter –

Unless...

"Anya?" Madeline's voice floated into the room. Anya heard her footsteps softly pad down the hall. She tapped at the door. "Are you feeling alright?" Madeline asked.

Anya hastily threw a robe over her nightdress and peeked her head out the door.

"I'm so sorry, Madeline," she said, forcing a smile. "I should have helped you, but I'm embarrassed to say I overslept."

Madeline took in the detritus in the room and looked at her friend. "The wind is howling this morning," Madeline said, rubbing her belly. "I'm surprised it didn't wake you."

Anya swallowed hard. "The wind soothes me sometimes. How are YOU feeling this morning?" Anya asked, extending a gentle hand to Madeline's arm.

"Well, I'll tell you – I'm glad the wind is soothing to you, because Baby here has been kicking me since the moonrise. I haven't been able to sleep a wink."

Anya frowned. "I am sorry, Madeline. Please – I'll be down in a second. Enjoy the morning alone with Caleb. I've intruded too many mornings. As soon as he goes off to work, I'll brew some tea for you and get you settled. It's the least I can do. You put your feet up and rest and I'll take care of what needs doing today."

"Madeline?"

Both women turned to the voice at the bottom the stairs

"I'm coming, Caleb!" The wind screeched against the house and the windowpanes rattled in their frames. "That soothes you?" asked Madeline, a wry smile on her face. "Well, take your time getting dressed. And if you don't mind, I would love a cup of tea after he leaves. You always brew the most soothing cups."

"Please tell Caleb goodbye from me."

"I will," Madeline said.

Anya shut the door and leaned against it, looking out at the black branches of the trees flailing in the wind.

She had to do something to ensure her father did not get a boat. Boats from St. John's to Montreal sailed every fortnight and one had just arrived yesterday.

Anya placed her face in her palms and rubbed her tired eyes. The delicate ring Liam had given her scratched at her cheekbone.

Married.

If they got married soon, this week, her father would have no reason to come. Already he would be fighting Mariloup and if they were already married… It was the only way. Liam would certainly agree. Wasn't he pushing for this wedding only last night? And he had the church ready – she would tell him. She would tell him today that she agreed. And if she asked, she was sure he could convince the priest to marry them this Saturday rather than next. She would talk to him – tonight, after dinner. They would walk, he would surely agree.

They would be married this week, no matter what.

"Goodbye, Anya!" Caleb's voice called up the stairs.

"Goodbye, Caleb!" she called back. "Be safe out there!"

CHAPTER THIRTY-NINE

"The wind." Caleb squinted out at the misty dawn and shook his head.

"It'll be fine," Liam said, shrugging his raincoat on and tossing a lobster cage to Caleb. "Come on."

"You know, you could at least thank a fellow," Caleb said.

Liam grinned. "Thank you. Now get in the boat."

Caleb sighed and pulled the cap down, shielding his eyes from the mist and drizzle. "How many do you need? You know, Madeline is home alone."

"We need a least a dozen. Madeline has at least a month left and besides, Anya is with her." Caleb grunted and grabbed an oar. "What?" Liam asked. "If you have something to say, say it."

Caleb put his palm out and shook his head. "No, no," he said. "I've got nothing."

"You obviously have something. If you need to say it then say it."

Caleb's brown eyes shifted down to the lobster cages and he leaned over to settle them more tightly in the hull. Again, he shook his head and shuddered against the spray of the ocean. Liam stopped rowing and stared him down until he had to meet his friend's eyes.

"What?" Liam asked. "You better just tell me or I'm shoving you out of this boat."

Slamming the last lobster trap down, Caleb looked up and shook his head. "Fine. You want to hear it? I have a pregnant wife at home. I'm out on a Sunday fishing again with you so you can have extra money to pay a priest to hurry up and marry a girl whose father, whose entire family, can't even be bothered to answer a letter. I mean – I like Anya – you know I do. But what do you know about her?"

"What do I know about her?" Liam asked, furrowing his brows. "What do I need to know about her? She's interesting, she's pretty, she has that beautiful voice. And she'll make a great wife -she obviously knows how to take care of people – she takes care of Madeline-"

"Exactly!" Caleb said, rowing harder. "Madeline. She just moved in with us and is staying with my wife, making teas and tinctures and God knows what else. Madeline says sometimes she hears her singing and chanting in the middle of the night."

"Chanting? What the hell do you mean?" Liam asked, leaning forward. "And you know, I'm sorry she's making teas and tinctures to help your wife feel better."

Caleb shook his head. "Fine. But what could have happened to a woman that she just up and moves to a big city? Who, for some reason, has no contact with her

173

family? Who would agree to live with… essentially strangers that she just met?"

"What are you saying?" Liam asked, his voice a low growl as his arms flexed taunt with rowing.

"I'm not saying anything – slow the damn boat down, Liam. You're not even watching where we're heading." Caleb shoved his oar backwards. "I'm asking. I'm just asking a question. What do you know about her? Why the rush to marry next weekend?"

"Why the rush?" Liam tilted his head and raised his eyebrows. Caleb couldn't help but smile a little at his friend's expression.

"Alright," he said. "I understand that rush. But Liam, really. Why next Sunday? Why not wait until you've heard from her father – from any of her family?"

Liam swallowed hard. He looked his friend hard in the eyes. "Because she asked. She came to me and asked. To get married as soon as possible. And when a woman you love asks that, you don't ask why."

"There are plenty of reasons to ask why," Caleb muttered.

"What was that?" The color was rising swiftly into Liam's face. "What are you suggesting?"

Caleb looked out to the waves which were splashing over the side of the boat now. "We should turn back," he said.

"I am not turning back!" Liam shouted. "I'm not turning back until we get these damn lobsters and you know what, I'm not turning my back on her."

"Liam. Calm down. Look at the damn weather – look at the clouds. It's not a good day."

"If you don't want to help me, that's fine. And if you're going to insult the woman I love, I'll take her out of your home today and put her up in a hotel. You know what? I'll do the fishing – just sit there." Liam picked up one of the cages and threw in into the choppy water. "You know we can only catch lobster in the morning. I know I can get my haul – the stupid lobster will be confused by the waves and if I wait until later, I really can't go. Just – you know what – just sit there. And if you have anything else to say about Anya, just shut your mouth."

Caleb clenched his teeth. He gazed out into the waves, seeing the swells growing taller and wider. There was something else about the waves too, something else he couldn't understand. Maybe a crosswind. Whatever it was, the odd shape of water was getting closer to the boat. They had to go back. He reached over and grabbed an oar. "Liam," he said gently. "Stop. I'm sorry I said anything. I will help you, but we need to go back. This is bad water."

Liam yanked a lobster cage up and counted under his breath. "I need two more. You can wait a few more goddamn minutes."

"I'll lend you the money," Caleb said. "Whatever you need. And I apologize."

"What is said can't be unsaid," Liam said through clenched teeth. "I'm doing this – I'll marry her. And I'm sorry you think she's – whatever you think she is."

"I don't think anything," Caleb said. "I've known you since we were boys, Liam. You do everything so damn hastily. And sometimes you don't think. And you take risks. Your dad wanted you to be part of the business and you're here instead doing what? Fishing? Riding around on horseback as a Mountie? Sometimes you have to just do the correct thing. Take part in the family business. Wait to marry a stranger you've known for a month. Listen to someone for once!"

"Wait to marry?" Liam shouted over the waves "Explain to me – how is it that Madeline is weeks from having a baby and you're still waiting to get married?"

Caleb reared up in the boat and lunged at Liam, his closed fist meeting Liam's right cheekbone. "That's my wife, you bastard! Now turn this goddamn boat around!"

Liam threw his oar down and reached for Caleb's collar. Suddenly, the boat keeled to the right and both men were thrown into the hull. Over the screeching of the wind and the holler of waves, they could hear a deep rumble, as if it came from the depths of the earth. Something lifted the hull of the boat again and water flooded in, washing three of the lobster cages out to sea.

Liam grabbed the side of the boat to steady himself and a fountain of water sprayed up from the ocean and soaked him. A black dappled mountain seemed to rise from the sea and suddenly in Liam's vision was nothing but black and grey.

"WHALE!" Caleb shouted.

Liam heard nothing but water. He saw the enormous fins as the humpback twirled her body and landed with a slam. Shuddering with fear, he tried to turn to see his friend, but found his neck wouldn't move. He tried to cry out, but his voice was paralyzed. He could only feel the rumbling and the lifting of the hull.

Caleb was screaming Liam's name, trying to pull him fully into the boat. "SHE'S STILL HERE!" Caleb shouted. "LIAM! GET IN THE BOAT. HOLD ON!" Liam heard nothing, only saw a mountain rising up again, and felt the back of the boat rear into the air. He was thrown down, but he saw the two fins rise as the whale lifted the boat and flipped onto her back, fins outstretched. He saw a something else too, something wet, green, fly through the air.

A bloodcurdling scream flew into his ears. The boat landed hard in the water, and suddenly, Liam could hear the wind, the waves crashing, the splintering of wood. He reached out, his arm moving again, throbbing in pain. He reached out for a handhold, for anything. His fingers found the dented lobster cage, the animal's shells cracked and liquid oozing out.

A rumble came from under the waves. Looking out, Liam saw a tail raise out of the water and slam down. And slip away.

Closer, there was something too. Floating toward him.

A green hat, soaking with water, crimson with blood.

CHAPTER FORTY

Anya stood at the prow of the ship as she sailed across the still waters. The night before held a flaming red sunset, causing Liam to squirm. It seemed like an accusation. The sailors, however, had relaxed their shoulders and taken a grateful glug out of their tankards. "Sailor's delight," they had said, cheering their glasses.

Anya moved to touch her new husband's arm in the sunset. He stiffened his muscles. "What is it?" she had asked.

Liam turned from the setting sun. "This is what the sky looked like that morning."

"The sunrise, you mean?" Anya asked.

"Yes."

"The sky was red in the morning?"

Liam let out a long sigh. "I knew better," he said.

Anya had stroked his arm gently. "It wasn't your fault."

"Anya, it's not helpful to talk about it anymore," Liam said, moving his arm from under her hand. "It's not helpful to hear you continue to speak of it." He shoved his hands in his coat pockets and turned away, walking down the deck.

This dawn, however, was a pinky-blue stillness, as if the aurora were holding her breath. As they sailed toward land, Anya could only see a shimmering cloud that indicated where the sky ended and the water began. She reached up and clasped her necklace in her hand, breathing deeply.

The shimmering became a pulsing, first in her palm and moving quickly behind her eyes. Anya felt the familiar shiver down her arms and through her torso, and she breathed in deeply. It was so easy to be overtaken by it and disappear into a swirl of colors and shapes only to emerge dizzy and unconnected. She felt the shimmering through her veins and whispered "Welcome" into the wind. Anchoring her feet to the deck of the ship, she sent the shimmering into her fingertips, drying the dew on the deck-rail as she did so. Next, she sent the shimmer through her head, and could feel the pulsing in her scalp. The wind encircled her face and lifted the tendrils of her hair so they brushed against her cheek.

"Tell me," Anya whispered, closing her eyes. "Please."

She felt a voice within the waves.

"Come. Build. Create."

That was what they planned to do, Anya thought, frustration creeping against the magic. This was not new information. And really, it was not what she was asking. She tried again.

"Tell me," she whispered, more firmly this time. "Why?"

The shimmering fell away and Anya felt a gripping around her heart, around her upper arms, below her belly. The stone on her necklace was cold and hard in her palm.

"Come. Build. Create."

Anya opened her eyes. The world stood still, no birds cawing, not even the splashing of waves against the hull of the ship, which continued her glide. The grip tightened around Anya's throat.

"It is not for you to ask." Anya felt the voice as her breath fell shallow and quick. "It is not for you to *tell*. Not for you to command." Anya's arms felt leaden as she gripped the rail harder. "Come. Build. Create."

Anya squeezed the stone in her palm as if to hurt it. She released the railing and took a shuddering breath, lifting her chin and opening her eyes. "Why do you *take?*" she hissed into the rising sun. "Why do you always take? It is for me to ask, and I will ask before I do anymore – before I fear anymore!"

"Land ho!" A shout from above startled Anya and she turned to see the sailor in the crows nest. Passengers came streaming onto the deck. She saw a man taller than the rest, holding a cup of tea and striding toward her. Anya smiled up at him and marched away from the prow, away from the rising sun.

She lifted her arms to circle his neck and kissed him. A long-buried grin spread across his face when she stepped off her tiptoes and took the tea from his hand. "Thank you," she said.

"For what?" Liam asked, looking into her dark, shining eyes.

"For a cup of tea. For a life."

Liam put his arm around her and pointed out toward the strip of land that was beginning to take shape in the distance. "There's a life," he said. "Yours and mine."

CHAPTER FORTY-ONE

The steamer floated up to the wooden dock and the deckhands scrambled deftly off to tie her up to the posts. The gangplank was lowered down and the passengers walked gamely down, legs buckling.

Anya wrapped her shawl more tightly around her shoulders, the wind was wet and cold.

Women in straw hats and full skirts stood waving on the shoreline, men in their suspenders holding pipes sat in chairs crafted from birch tree branches. Children with bare feet and sandy curls scampered up and down the dock, gawping at the newcomers. Liam raised his hand to shield his eyes as he looked for his contact from the Lighthouse. No one came forward, no one held a sign. Anya gripped her carpetbag tightly and looked up at her new husband. The band of gold shone on her hand. They stepped aside into the grassy field at the end of the dock. Anya ran her hand over the enormous plant with purple berries that reached almost to her shoulder.

"Those look ripe," Liam said.

"Don't." Anya shook her head. "Pokeweed."

Liam grinned and moved to pick it. "Should I poke you with it then?"

Anya brushed his hand away. "Don't touch it and don't eat it either. It's poisonous. In the spring when it's slight and vulnerable you can cook and eat the leaves, but when it's at it's full beauty... It'll attract the butterflies and all the pretty silly things, but if you let it touch your lips, it will kill you."

"Hmmm," Liam said. "Well, we don't need that." He put his suitcase into the grass. "We do need somewhere to stay. I need a warm bath and a cold drink. I don't know where Mr. Niedzvich is, but I know there's an inn a few miles north of here." He looked down at Anya's tiny, heeled boots with the buttons that reached her shin. "Can you walk in those?"

"I guess I'll have to," Anya said. Liam took her carpetbag in his free hand and Anya reached up to pull his jacket from where it was tucked on his elbow. She lifted his smaller case and threw his jacket around her shoulders, setting down the path of sweet grasses and prickly purple flowers. The warm, fading summer sun warmed their faces and eventually they came upon a huge white stone building with black framed windows and a tower rising from the center. It was bigger than any home or structure in Anya's town, and yet more quaint than most buildings she had learned to know in Montreal. A sign out front read "Hotel Uigge."

Liam held the big wooden door open for her and they strode to the front desk. Liam gave their name to the red-haired attendant, whose blue eyes brightened as she saw Liam's approach, and brightened even more as she read the name. Liam flashed a smile in response and Anya shook her head and smiled ruefully. She may have married the friendliest big bear of a man on earth. The now-blushing attendant handed Liam an envelope and said, "He's waiting for you in the restaurant, Mr. Leighton."

Before Liam could remember to introduce Anya, a booming voice echoed through the stone hallway.

"Mr. Leighton! We are thrilled you're here!

CHAPTER FORTY-TWO

"You'll be running the lighthouse," Mr. Niedzvich said, clapping Liam on the shoulder.

"The lighthouse?" Liam repeated, placing his hand on the chair in front of him.

"Of course. That's the job your friend applied for, the one he couldn't be bothered to show up to do."

Liam's hand on the chair began to shake, and his face lost color. Anya saw the now-familiar expression cross his broad features, the eyes going dark and his lips clenched tightly together. "My friend is dead."

Anya put a hand on Liam's arm. "He died tragically," she said. "In a boating accident, Mr... I'm sorry, I didn't catch your name."

Mr. Niedzvich painted on a kind smile. "Niedzvich. Albert Niedzvich." He clapped his hands together and straightened his shoulders. "Well, if only your friend had a lighthouse to guide him to shore," he said. "It sounds like fate, you taking his place."

Liam was silent, his knuckles white as he gripped the chair.

"Mr. Niedzvich, I'm Mrs. Leighton," Anya said quickly. "Would you be so kind as to show us to our house? It's been a long day."

"House?" Mr. Niedzvich looked at the two of them. "I thought your friend would have made it clear – well, perhaps he didn't tell you before he passed – the keeper of the lighthouse lives in the lighthouse."

"Now wait just a minute," Liam said, his voice shaking. "This posting clearly said a house was included. I've brought a wife; Caleb was going to bring his – " He stopped, swallowing hard. "His child. And his wife. You wrote specifically saying that the job came with a house."

Niedzvich put his hands up. "I wrote no such letter, Mr. Leighton. I don't do the writing here -that's our secretary. He makes mistakes, lots of them, poor fellow, but you know, you have a home within the lighthouse. A home that will suit you for years to come. It's cozy, I grant you, but for the two of you it will suit just fine."

"This was not the agreement," Liam said, his voice growing loud enough that patrons in the lobby turned.

"This is what is here," Niedzvich said. "But, you are in a place with plenty of natural resources, plenty of timber. And you look handy. I'm sure if it doesn't suit, the two of you will be able to build something all your own."

"With what money?" Liam slammed his fist on the chair.

"Again, Mr. Leighton, I can't take responsibility for that."

Anya stepped in front of her husband. "Thank you, Mr. Niedzvich. Liam, I think we should see the Lighthouse. Could we go now, Mr. Niedzvich?"

"Well, yes, of course," Niedzvich said, clearly trying to calm his temper. "I hoped we might want to have a drink together first, you know, perhaps a bite to eat. After all, my hope here is to be your family away from family."

Now it was Anya's turn to swallow hard. "I'm… quite tired. I appreciate the thought, but I would rather take a rest." Liam looked at her with concern.

"Of course, of course," Niedzwich said. "It's just a brisk walk, but it would take about an hour… should I get my cart?"

"We are not walking an hour," Liam said tersely. "It would be good if you got your cart."

"Certainly, certainly. I'll just settle my bill, and you can meet me out front." He ambled away, running his hand back through his balding hair.

Liam turned to Anya. "You're not feeling well?"

Anya looked up at him, eyes sparking with energy. "I'm perfectly alright, why?"

"You just said you were tired," Liam said.

"I only said that to end that conversation," she said.

"That man - what an absolute…" Liam balled his fists.

"He's not that bad," Anya said.

"Not that bad? Not that bad?" Liam asked. "He's an absolute fool! Thinking he can bring us here, promising a house and telling us we have to sleep in one room in a lighthouse?"

"We don't know if it's one room," Anya said.

"Why are you sticking up for him?" Liam asked.

"I'm not – I think we should just see and make the best of it."

"My God, what if it was Madeline in your place with a baby?"

Anya looked away, refusing to let the tears that flew to her eyes sneak out. Mariloup's voice hissed in her mind even now. "You can never give him a child. You're broken, like your mother."

"Anya…" Liam began.

"Well, Mr. Leighton, Mrs. Leighton!" the booming voice broke in. "Let's continue on to the lighthouse! Your new home."

CHAPTER FORTY-THREE

It had been two months. Anya and Liam were barely on speaking terms in the small cottage – if you could call it a cottage. There was no proper indoor stove; Anya had been doing her best to prepare meals over an outdoor fire, in the cold of January. She had felt sick to her stomach and exhausted for about a week, which she attributed to the grueling work and subpar food she had set on their table.

Liam had tried to remain cheerful and Anya had tried to rise to his attitude and be grateful for what she did have: a loving husband, a roof over her head, and meals… if they could be called that.

But it felt as if in this grand adventure, she had lost herself. She had no family, no friends, no job, nor any way to exercise her skills in embroidery, jewelry-making, or music. Those required an expense that was simply not feasible on a lightkeeper's salary. She did not even have a way to contact Aunt Airmed. Her letters had gone unanswered.

When they left Montreal after their subdued and tiny wedding, she had been prepared to struggle. After all, didn't they deserve some hardship, at the very least? Anya placed her hand on the small of her back as she thought of this long-held dream... of a grand, unknowable adventure with a man she loved...

But this adventure had no song.

She sighed heavily and ignored the rustle of paper from across the room. She did not see Liam look up from the Gazette with guilt in his eyes. She only heard his question.

"What's for supper?"

Suddenly, the pain in her back and belly, the pain in her head from hard work, and the ache in her heart for all those parts of her that were unreachable in this cottage at the end of the world flooded through her and she whipped around.

"I. have. No. idea."

Liam's eyes flickered from hurt into defense in a blink. "I only asked a question," he said, raising the paper back up to his face. "I should be able to ask my wife a question."

"It wasn't a question," snapped Anya. "It was a demand."

Liam slapped the paper down on his knee. "When did I – "

"What's for supper?" Anya asked, mockingly. "What do you think is for supper? The same supper that we've had for weeks: potatoes, broth, a bit of that dried

191

venison that smells like an old shoe – the only thing we have to make over our 'fire,'" she said. "Outside. In the snow."

"I'm sorry that this," Liam gestured around the room, "Isn't good enough for you," he said. "But I'm trying."

The fire flashing in Anya's eyes dimmed just slightly as she saw the sadness on her husband's gaunt face. She wanted to go to him, wrap herself in his long arms and sink her head in his chest, but the anger and sadness flooding in her heart kept her frozen in place. She needed someone to blame for all of this, and he was the only person for miles. So, he would have to feel her wrath, even if she kept herself from verbalizing it.

Anya dropped her gaze and gave another heavy sigh. Turning from her husband, she gathered up the sliced potatoes from the tiny table into a wooden bowl, lifted her shawl over her head, and walked out the door into the blustery winter wind.

CHAPTER FORTY-FOUR

Anya went out into the yard where the fire guttered in the stone pit. She blew on her hands in their tattered knitted gloves. Anger boiled in her heart as she picked up the dried piece of driftwood she used to stoke the flames. It wasn't fair. She hadn't agreed to this; this life of isolation, of emptiness. When they had sailed to America, struggle had seemed like a noble adventure, and maybe it was because she had never known struggle. She had not known cold like this, nor the bite of hunger in her belly. There had always been flour and fire, spices and thread and yarn. Of course, they had all worked hard, but there had been the songs of her mother and her aunt, the beautiful and mystical designs in the silver they worked, the flowers and swirls and the words in the language of another time that appeared in the handkerchiefs and blankets her mother embroidered. There had been her father, quiet but content in the worn armchair, her friends in the village, there had been...

...him.

His blazing eyes, his music, his talk of dreams and adventure. His calloused hands on the soft skin of her cheek. His berry-colored lips on hers…

She shook her head and clenched her jaw. She shouldn't think of that time – it was gone. He destroyed it. And to think of him and Hannah, of the baby… that thought hurt physically. The pain in her chest when she imagined Cillian holding a baby in his arms, a baby that wasn't hers. The pain in her belly, her empty belly, that carried no new life despite their weekly coupling.

What was she doing? What was she doing here in this wilderness, far from anything and anyone she knew? What was she doing with this man who said he loved her, but if she was being truthful with herself, she barely knew? Liam was kind, and he worked hard to be sure, but where was the life he promised, that her aunt told her to live, that her mother dreamed for her? Where was the life she had promised herself?

Tears streamed from her eyes and settled, frozen and tight on her pale cheeks. Icy wind blew around her sodden skirt, but could not lift the ends. Her hand reached up instinctively to touch her necklace. Maybe if she… it had been so long since she had brewed the tea, had closed her eyes and breathed deeply and waited for the guidance of the Divine. She had only heard her own voice and Liam's. Perhaps if she sought to hear the voice of someone, something more powerful… Anya squeezed her eyes shut and reached her free hand into her pocket where she still placed the bag of sacred stones each morning. The other hand gripped her jasper pendant. She raised her eyes to the gray sky and took a deep breath.

"What am I doing?" she whispered to the wind. "What do I do?" She squeezed her eyes shut, trying to reach something, something beyond the icy air that surrounded her. "What more can I do?" she asked. The old familiar shiver began to flow through her veins and she welcomed it, a great relief flooding her. A picture began to form behind her eyelids, lilac and lavender, like the sky when she arrived. A pulsing tightness vibrated through her body, and she felt a heaviness and a shelter combined as one. Something that enclosed her, sparkling, safe and warm. Anya breathed again and tightened her grip on the jasper.

"What do I do?" she asked in her mind, separated too far from the world now to speak aloud. "What am I forgetting?" Swirls and shapes spun in her mind's eye, and she began to lose the feeling of cold in her feet, on her fingertips. She began to live in this glimpse of Beyond. She could hear the music, great music, tunes that seemed eternal whispered on the wind.

"Anya!"

The sound arched her back and snapped her eyes open. Whose voice? Who had reached to her from the swirling eddies?

"Anya?"

She turned to the sound of the voice. Liam stood in the open doorway, looking at her with anxious eyes.

Anya met his gaze for a second and then closed her eyes in resignation. He had called her back. Called her from the answer she sought, from the Something that spoke to her, from the beauty that used to be woven into her daily life. Now there was only this. Biting cold, gray skies, dirty snow. A guttering fire.

An empty belly.

"I thought you were stoking the fire," Liam said, rubbing his hands together against the cold. "Didn't you say we needed to have supper?"

This was who she was. This was reality. She was not some blessed descendant from a mysterious Island of gilded stones. She was not an artisan with a needle and thread or a singer of ancient melodies. Nor was she gifted for forging, nor for Seeing, but to make a gruel to sustain herself and this man she had promised her life to. She was a gaunt woman standing in wilderness trying to make a fire. Her mother was dead, gone. Not to be heard from in some vision or through a swirl of color. Her father was effectively gone. No letters had been answered, probably the doing of Mariloup. Her aunt was lost to her; Anya was forbidden to return to the Island. And Cillian… was in the arms of another, surrounded, Anya imagined, by raven-haired children and music.

She had made choices, Anya told herself. No one had done this to her, no one had forced her. She had placed herself here. It was just her. Her choices. She had been too afraid at every turn to reach for the magic, to reach for the music. She had taken the path usually traveled by all.

And she was here. In this cold dirty snow, with a hungry man waiting for his supper. She lowered her eyes to the guttering flames and said, "I'll make it."

Liam looked at the set of her shoulders and noted her quiet voice. He furrowed his brows. He supposed it was better than the anger that had welled up within her when she stormed out of the house. But still… he didn't know what to do to help, to make her smile, and it made him feel more helpless than he already did. "Do you want my coat?" he asked.

Anya raised her eyes to him. Their emptiness sent a shiver down his spine. "I am Cold," she said.

"I know," Liam said, "That's why I'm offering my _"

Anya put up a hand to cut off his words. "No. This is my… this is my choice."

Liam took a step out onto the porch. "Anya, you're not yourself," he said. "I think you should come inside."

Anya felt the last of the shivering pulse of anger, of Spirit, leave her. She felt only the cold icy wind and saw Liam's tall frame stooped halfway out of the doorway. She saw his stockinged feet advancing in the snow on the porch and knew that drying socks would be one more thing on her unending list.

"Liam, go inside. You'll hurt your feet walking without your boots."

"I'm just trying to help," he said.

Anya forced a smile. Liam winced at its falsehood. "I know," she said. "I promise I'll… I'll get this fire going. I'll be inside in a moment."

Liam gave her a searching look and she held his gaze with blank eyes. Finally, he nodded and ducked back inside the door.

Anya released the grip she held on to the pendant and picked up the piece of driftwood. Carefully, she stirred the coals and coaxed them until they glowed. Marching through the snow to the woodpile, she selected the drier logs and brushed off the dusting of snow. When she placed the last one on the fire, something caught, and flames shot into the air. Anya jumped back and waved her hands in her face to chase away the cinders. The back of her fingers caught on something sitting on the bodice of her cloak and she made to brush it away, thinking it was another hot ash.

Something snapped.

With wide eyes, Anya watched as her pendant flew through the air, passed through the rising flames and landed across the fire pit in the snow. She scrambled around the pit and dug furiously. Finally, after what felt like hours, the sunlight caught a dull shimmer next to a stone jutting out of the ground. She snatched up the object and opened her palm. In in, sat the silver setting and half the stone. The crack ran along the diagonal, ragged and crumbled. Panic welled up as she dug furiously for the other part of the stone. It could be fixed, she was sure. With paste, with a mixture, with something. Tears flowed down her face again as she looked, cold fingers scratching at the hard dirt beneath the frost. Finally, with a shuddering sigh, she sat up.

It was gone.

That life she knew, the life she was raised in, the life she dreamed of, was gone. There was only the life she lived now. The life she had chosen.

Swallowing a sob, she placed the silver setting with its half stone in her pocket. It knocked against the bag of Spirit Stones she carried every day.

With a ragged yell, Anya ripped the sack from the pocket of her dress. She dug the stones of their embroidered bag and stared at them. "Protection." "Grounding." "Safety." "Freedom." They sparkled even in the stingy January light, but that's all they were, stones. Nothing, with no real meaning. She stared into the woods and heard the crashing waves from the lake beyond.

Stones. Weighing her down. With a shriek, she lifted her arm and threw them into the empty meadow beyond the cabin.

They landed in the snow without a sound.

Anya pulled her shawl around her head and turned from the water; turned from the wind. She had to make gruel to feed their bodies, but she, Anya, was already gone.

CHAPTER FORTY-FIVE

A dash of green appeared under Liam's boot as he walked out into the snow with an axe over his shoulder. Their shack had lasted them through the winter, but barely. The light in his wife's eyes had almost completely dimmed. More than that, she had been resting after supper every day for the past month, complaining of head pains, stomach pains, back pains. Her cheeks were flushed constantly but her skin was as cold as the air, no sign of fever. She had even stopped brewing that tea she drank every day, the one she said was handed down to her from her Aunt. She said she couldn't stomach it. Liam noticed she couldn't even stomach breakfast most days.

Grimacing, he recalled the day in January when she had come in, almost frozen, cups of gruel in each cracked hand. "It's gone," was all she would say. Eventually, he got an answer out of her. She meant the necklace, the one he had pulled out of the water in a time that seemed eons ago. It was broken, lying somewhere in the snow.

Well, perhaps when the snow finally thawed, he would find it for her. Repair it for her somehow.

Repair… all of this, any of it. But to begin, they needed a better dwelling. He turned his eyes to the forest's edge, scanning the hardwoods. He looked at the maples, the white and black papered birches, knotted eyes of the beech trees. What he needed was pine, or better yet, oak. Liam sighed, it was taking ages to fell the trees needed to build Anya a proper homestead.

The drumming beat of a mallard's wings shook the quiet air. Liam smiled. Birds. Despite everything, despite his failings, Spring would come whether he was ready or not. He wished he had thought to bring his rifle for a bit of fresh meat for dinner. He turned to see where the bird flew; perhaps he could come back tomorrow. As he stepped away from the forest toward the sound of the mallard, his boot caught something solid, and he stumbled. Shooting pain flew through his knee and up his leg. Liam swore as he sat down hard in the snow, grabbing his knee. After the first pains subsided, he flexed it slightly, trying to discern the immediate pain from true hurt. The knee bent and he rubbed a gloved hand over his trousers, which had torn. Liam took a swallow of whiskey from his flask. How could he trip on the hard earth? And come to that, Spring was coming; it was April after all. Should the earth soften just a little by know?

He reached to brush the snow off the earth that had felled him and touched something more solid, more convex than earth should ever be. Speckled ochre, ruby, and ebony shone through the snow. The dim sunlight caught a pearlescent streak and made it shine. Liam knelt on his good knee and brushed further with both hands – it was a stone. A stone the size of a young child.

Granite.

Surely he would have known in the autumn when they arrived on the Peninsula if a stone of this magnitude had been sitting yards from his front door. Liam rose up to walk and measure the true size of the stone and his heel hit another solid surface. He turned backward, eyes wide, kicking the white flakes off what was a rose-colored, banded stone. Huge. It would take two men to lift it. Liam began walking, carefully but quickly, his boots slipping as the terrain lifted in small, hard hills. He kicked the snow, brushed it off and used the top of his axe to hit the earth. A clear ring shot into the air. Time after time, the top edge of the axe slammed into stone, each strike ringing like a bell.

Liam began to laugh in disbelief. He could not countenance it. True, they had not had time to explore or prepare the land in the autumn before the frost, but surely, surely they would have noticed a field full of stones. Liam struck the top of his axe to a smooth, saffron colored stone the size of his head. Enough to build a fence, enough to build…

"What song is that?"

A clear voice rang out from the porch. Liam turned to see Anya wrapped in a shawl, face pale in the morning light.

"Do you hear those bells?" Anya called to him. "What song are they playing?"

Liam grinned at her and the excitement in his blue eyes made a faint warmth flow through her. She could help smiling herself. She hadn't seen that man since the night he proposed, the night of the pub, since before the ocean waves took...

"It's not a bell," Liam shouted back, still grinning. "But sure as rain, it is a song!"

PART III

CHAPTER FORTY-SIX

Anya closed the heavy wooden door of the stone house and wiped her brow. "Wait, Nellie!" she called. "I can't move so fast with Isla on my hip." The pink-cheeked little girl reached up a sticky hand and wound her fingers around a lock of hair that had escaped Anya's chignon. She smiled down at the little girl and gently loosed her hand, kissing it. "What's there, Isla? Honey from your morning bun?"

"Sa-sa!" the toddler said, pointing her hand out toward the horizon. Anya took a deep breath and began to walk faster. "We'll catch your big sister, don't worry."

Keeping the two blonde braids with their violet bows in her sights, Anya walked along the farmland. She could see the houses of her neighbors; see the smoke rising from stone chimneys. Liam had built so many of them; he had even built the church. After that February day three years ago when he had found the stones in the ground, he had been working non-stop. He worked so hard that she barely saw him. A group of young men from the village helped him harvest stone, and he had recruited another group of builders. When he wasn't in a field or a worksite, he was having a pint on someone's porch. He came home late each night, contented and exhausted. He would inhale his supper, kiss his children, tossing them in the air to make them squeal with laughter. They adored him, worshipped him, really. And after he wound them into balls of hysterical energy, he would fall asleep, most usually on the sofa.

These days, they had enough money for needles and thread, enough for meat and provisions from the market. The stone house was cozy and warm in the winter, and in the summer, Anya could throw open the glass windows to watch the breeze rustle the curtains she had made.

There was money for yarn, although not embroidery thread. In her spare moments, Anya would crochet blankets, always in bright colors of sunrise, or the deep blues of the lake and sky. She kept her pieces on top of the wardrobe, high above where little fingers could reach them. It was nothing close to what she was capable of; the fine stitching and embroidery taught to her by her mother and aunt could not be done without silken embroidery thread, which was beyond their means. She took in sewing and repairs for some of the men in the village who had settled without wives, and made a pittance to add to the family income.

What she missed the most though, was the silver-smithing. Liam had promised last Christmas that he would build her a shed and send for a forge. He had even wrapped the corner stone stones in brown paper and put them under the tree for her to unwrap. She had been overwhelmed with joy and gratitude, tears falling down her cheeks for the first time since that awful day in the snow.

But it had been six months, and he had yet to place the stones. Other people's homes and needs always seemed to come first, and since the building work brought in much more income than her sewing, there wasn't much to say about it.

"Nellie," she called again, closer now, close enough to reach her if she ran. Nellie turned toward her mother, holding a black and white speckled hen with a red comb.

"Chicky laid eggs!" The child dropped the bird to the ground without ceremony and pointed to the wooden henhouse.

"Good," said Anya said. "That's her job."

"Eggs is chicky's job," the little girl repeated. "Papa's job is building the town."

"You're right, little one," Anya said, lifting a corner of her apron to wipe a spot of dirt off of her daughter's bright face. "Everyone must have a job. We help one another by doing our jobs."

"My job is to take care of Chicky."

"And you do lovely work," Anya said, tucking a loose curl behind the little girl's cheek as the toddler wriggled on her hip. "Although you might like to set her down more gently."

"And!" Nellie continued, finger in the air. "Mama's job is cleaning the floor and cooking the porridge."

Anya grimaced. Her mind raced back to blankets rich with meadows of embroidered flowers, and grinding stones until she had brought out their inner beauty. She thought of shaping and tracing the molten metals into swirls and eddies. And she thought of the wooden floor of their stone house. It needed scrubbing once again from the honey-covered bun that Isla had dropped on the floor that morning. The insects were fierce on this peninsula, and if she didn't get to it soon, there would be a parade of ants through her kitchen.

"Come, Nellie. We need to get back."

"I get Chicky's eggs!" Nellie said, loosening her hand from her mother's grip and running toward the coop. A swell of emotion welled up in Anya, a fierce pride in her daughter's spirit, her quickness and her intelligence. And smaller, but still present, she felt an ache of jealousy for Nellie's freedom.

"Be careful," Anya called as little Isla squirmed on her hip. "Don't stray too far. There might be bad animals trying to get into the coop."

Nellie turned to her mother and stomped a foot. "I will beat them," she said, and marched into the chicken coop.

CHAPTER FORTY-SEVEN

Liam stepped inside the threshold and grinned at what he found there. His eldest daughter was playing with the wooden blocks he had carved, and his younger daughter was knocking them over, causing both children to laugh wildly. He could smell the beef and vegetable stew on the stove and his stomach grumbled in gratitude. Anya's slight frame was bent over the floor, her backside rocking back and forth as she scrubbed. His smile spread farther at the sight and blood rushed through his veins. He unlaced his boots and stepped toward his wife, yearning to give her a kiss on her tanned neck, yearning to give her more…

As he tiptoed up to her and bent over, he felt a hard squeeze on his leg.

"Papa!" Nellie squealed. Patting Anya on her backside, Liam turned toward his daughter and lifted her high in the air.

"There's my girl!" he said, giving her a spin. She shrieked in delight as Isla hooted and cooed in her corner, bouncing up and down, begging in her baby way to be picked up too.

"Young Madam!" Liam's booming voice resounded through the house as he set Nellie down. He clapped his big hands together and wriggled Isla out of the chair, setting her on his knee and bouncing her. Still grinning at his children, he called to Anya. "How about a treat for this young lady, Mama?"

Anya rubbed at the headache that was starting to build behind her eyes. The sharp cleaning liquid dried her hands until they were cracked and made her head split if she used it too often. It grated her nerves when Liam called her "Mama." She was not his mother. She was a mother, yes, but only to these two babies, and not every hour of every day. The guilt struck through her once again. How could she feel anything but honored by the designation "Mother" when it was what her own mother wished for so desperately. What Anya had always thought might never come for her.

The headache began to pulse. "They've had enough treats," she snapped, more sharply than she'd meant to. She gave a big sigh, trying to relax her shoulders, relax her neck. "Would you like tea and a biscuit, Liam?"

Liam's grin had faded at her sharp tone. "I was only happy to see everyone at the end of a long day."

"I know," Anya said. "We're happy to see you too."

"It doesn't seem like it," Liam muttered, setting the baby down, who immediately began to squall. Anya walked over to pick her up, raising her face to Liam for a kiss. Instead of planting a lingering kiss on her lips as he usually did, he pecked her cheek and made for the back door. "I'll just go wash my hands," he said. "It was a long day today. The granite for the Conorach's house was rough and heavy." He turned back to her. "And yes, tea and a biscuit would be fine. If it's not too much to ask." Anya heard the hint of petulance in his tone and rolled her eyes. It shouldn't be like this, she thought. It didn't used to be. What was it about her that irritated him so?

When he came back into the room, she placed a steaming cup of tea in front of him and a plate of freshly baked biscuits, slathered with extra butter and honey, hoping the extravagance might show him she cared. That she was sorry for... being always so tired and irritated at the mundanity of the days.

"Biscuits! Biscuits! Biscuits!" Nellie scampered into her father's lap and snatched a biscuit off the plate, scattering honey-soaked crumbs all over the sofa and floor.

"Nellie, those are your father's biscuits," Anya scolded. "He's worked hard all day, and he needs something to eat."

"I work hard all this day too," Nellie said, raising her blonde eyebrows. "Papa, I got Chicky's egg! And I carried it back to the house for Mama!"

The sound of Liam's laughter melted some of the tension out of the room. "Well, that sounds like hard work, my little Nellie. You've certainly earned a biscuit. Now finish that up without making too much of a mess. I need to give something to your mother." Liam popped another biscuit in his mouth and brushed the crumbs off his hands as he stood up.

"Mr. Conorach was so impressed with the stones I found for his entryway that he gave me something his wife had left over from the last shipment," Liam said, taking a package wrapped in brown paper out of his jacket pocket and handing it to Anya.

She wiped her hands on her apron and looked at him in surprise. "Thank you," she said, her voice deep and gentle.

"Well don't thank me until you open it," Liam said, wanting to reach out and brush the errant hair back from her face. He wasn't yet sure if his touch would be welcome. "It could be a skunk pelt for all I know."

Anya chuckled ruefully. "Let's hope not." She untied the string and carefully unfolded the paper to reveal a bolt of sunshine yellow silk. Brushing her fingertips over it, she gave a gasp of delight. It had been years since she had seen or touched anything so beautiful.

"You keep saying our quilt is tattered beyond repair," Liam said, shoving his hands in his pockets. "I thought you might make a cover..." He struggled to find the right word.

"A coverlet," Anya said softly. She lifted her hazel eyes to him. "Yes, I could."

"Or some dresses for the girls," Liam stammered. "Whatever you wanted."

"A coverlet for us sounds perfect," Anya said. "I could embroider it – "

"Well, that's what I thought," Liam said quickly. "And I can pick you up some thread at the General Store tomorrow. If you tell me the colors."

"I'll go," Anya said. "Liam…" She reached out and took her husband's hand. "Thank you."

*   *   *

That evening after the children were finally settled, Liam poured each of them a strong draught of his good scotch. By the morning, the quilt on their bed was well and truly tattered beyond repair.

CHAPTER FORTY-EIGHT

Leaving Isla in the pram outside, Anya tightened her grip on Nellie's hand as she pushed open the screen door of the General Store. She barely registered Nellie's persistent exclamations about and requests for barley sugars, caramels, and taffy that lay so temptingly in the wooden barrels. She repeated over and over, "Yes, I see them sweetheart. No, you must wait until I have picked out my thread. No, you may not touch." Anya greeted the proprietor of the store with a quiet nod and a patient smile as he waxed poetic about Liam and all the hard work he was doing. "We're very grateful to him," Anya said, pink rushing up her cheeks as the memory of the night before flooded her memory.

"As you should be," nodded Mr. Doyle. "He's a hard worker and a fine fellow. Now, you must have come in here for something other than to spin the yarn with me," he said.

"In fact, I've come for embroidery thread," Anya said, a smile pulling at her lips.

"Ah, how lovely," Mr. Doyle pointed. "Just to the back there. And Young Miss must have some barley sugars on the way out." Nellie widened her enormous blue eyes and flashed him a grin. "What a beautiful child," Mr. Doyle said. "Your family must be touched by something sweeter than most. Go on now, Mrs. Leighton. The barley sugars will be on the house today."

"What do you say, Nellie?" Anya prompted.

"Fank you," Nellie whispered, hopping up and down.

"After Mama picks out some thread for the coverlet." Anya led Nora to the back of the shop and spent a glorious few moments fingering violet, cerulean, and peridot silk thread, twisting the string around her fingers and holding it to the sunlight. She wished she had brought a snippet of the silk with her to match the thread, but she didn't dare waste a scrap. Checking the prices of the skeins carefully and trying to ignore the pit in her stomach over their cost, Anya heard a shrill laugh from the front of the store.

"Well, what a pretty girl we have here!" the voice said. Anya set the thread down and pasted on a smile for her neighbor. "You take right after your handsome father," Mrs. Conorach said, stroking Nellie's curls. "Blonde hair and blue eyes, as bright as the summer sky!"

"What do you say, Nellie?" Anya prompted again, setting the thread down.

"Fank you fank you," Nellie yelped, grinning.

"Nellie, please go wait on the bench outside," Anya said. "Check on Isla, and sit still."

"Good morning, Anya," Mrs. Conorach said brightly, her full chest popping out of her bright yellow silk dress, her tiny waist cinched tightly. "You must be here to pick out some thread to make a dress of your own, or one for your sweet daughter."

"Hello, Mrs. Conorach," Anya said, with one eye on her daughter who was now skipping through the store. "Thank you so much for the material. It's absolutely beautiful."

"Oh it's no trouble at all! Liam has been working so hard on our house, and he found the most perfect stones to frame the porch. Granite, he said, but I just said they were as pink as a rose and perfectly suited. I love pink, I told him, I simply love it. And he's charming, Anya, we chatted all through tea."

"Did you?" Anya asked.

"Oh yes, he chats as long as the day is long. I'm sorry if I – if we kept him a little too late. It's just that Mr. Conorach certainly needs to chat, and Liam is such a fun-loving man. Anyway, I know that I've been keeping him from you and you're way out on the end of the road. You're so attentive with your darling daughters that we hardly see you. So I said to him, Anya must have the rest of this silk. To sew a dress. Do you know – you should get some lace for it too!" Mrs. Conorach plucked at the lace on her sleeves. "They don't have it here of course, you have to go to the city, but I'm making Mr. Conorach take me there next week. You should join us!"

"Thank you, I don't know if I could leave the girls. As you point out, Liam works such long hours…"

"Oh, your children could stay with my children. My eldest is seven; surely she could watch Nellie and the baby."

"And I don't believe our budget quite stretches to lace."

Mrs. Conorach pulled her head back. "Well, we will just have to increase Liam's fees, won't we?"

"Mrs. Conorach," Anya said, "That's not at all what I meant…"

A large crash could be heard at the front of the store followed by a piping soprano voice. "Oopsie budaisy!"

"Excuse me," Anya said, rushing to find Nellie by an overturned barrel of caramels. She yanked her up by her arm. "I told her to wait and to sit still!" Anya whispered fiercely in the child's ear, her worry and humiliation turning to anger at the child.

"Oh it's nothing a little help can't fix." Mrs. Conorach bent down and shoveled the caramels into the barrel with Anya and Nellie, who was pouting at her mother's harsh tone. "Here, sweetie," Mrs. Conorach unwrapped a caramel and popped it into Nellie's mouth with her lace-gloved hands. She rose and turned to the storekeeper. "Put four caramels on my tab, Mr. Doyle." Turning, she pressed three more candies into Nellie's hand. "Have one more, give one to Sister, and don't forget to save the last sweet for your papa when he returns from our house this afternoon."

Anya clenched her jaw. "What do you say, Nellie?" she asked.

"Fank you," Nellie said, her little lip still trembling. Anya swallowed hard and placed the last of the caramels into the barrel. She stood and looked Sylvie Conorach in the eye.

"Thank you for your generosity, Mrs. Conorach," she said.

"Oh, it's my pleasure," Sylvie said, bustling out of the store. "I'll make sure Liam comes home at a decent time tonight. Well, as decent of a time as we can spare him!" Her laugh fluttered through the air. She flounced out the door, but not before turning to say, "Plan for next week! Our trip to town for lace!"

The screen door slammed, and Anya heard Mrs. Conorach coo at Isla in her pram. Nellie looked up at her mother.

"Mrs. Leighton?" The storeowner called. "I've got that embroidery floss all wrapped and ready to go."

Anya walked toward the counter. "That was so kind, Mr. Doyle. And thank you. We are so sorry about the caramels."

"Don't give it another thought," the older man said. "Children are children. If I didn't want them to feel welcome in here, I wouldn't put candy by the door. Of course it's tough on you mothers, I know, but I just can't resist seeing their happiness." He held her gaze. "It's an easy happiness for children, isn't it?"

"Yes," Anya said. Clearing her throat, she pulled out her purse and asked, "How much do we owe you?"

Mr. Doyle brushed his hand through the air. "I've put it on your tab. And Mrs. Leighton?" He handed her the package and patted her hand. "A boat is coming into port this Friday. It's carrying fresh supplies and stories from the sailors and who knows what all. Perhaps it carries some new happiness for us grown folk too."

CHAPTER FORTY-NINE

As promised, Mrs. Conorach had Liam home by suppertime that evening. Anya saw them walking down the hill together, and she noticed the smile on her husband's face, his easy gait. It reminded her of walks along the river back in Canada. It reminded her of the night she sang in the pub with him as he played the fiddle. A fiddle that by all accounts was languishing in the rafters. It reminded her of a time filled with music.

Now the only sounds she could hear were the flutelike tones of Mrs. Conorach's bright voice and Liam's hearty laughter. Anya looked in the mirror and the face that looked back at her was thin. Her hazel eyes were dull with tiredness and had blueish bags underneath. Taking a deep breath, she pinched her cheeks to coax some color into them and smoothed back her hair into a plain chignon. She fluffed her worn indigo skirt and walked out onto the porch, crossing her arms against the evening chill. She forced a smile and waved to Liam and Sylvie Conorach, who were close enough to look up and see her. But neither of them glanced her way.

Nellie ran through the meadow just then, a posy of wildflowers clutched in her hand. She crashed into Liam's leg, but he barely looked at his daughter, still talking and laughing. Finally, Mrs. Conorach bent down and touched the flowers. "Well, Miss Nellie! Lovely to see you again, dear."

"Fank you!" Nellie said, bouncing up and down and reaching her arms up for her father. Sylvie picked her up instead and waved at Anya. She carried the girl up the steps and set her down, turning to smile at Liam who loped up the steps after her.

"You see, Anya, I told you we'd have him home in time. Do you know, Nellie, my Christian name is Sylvie. And we both have golden hair. Nellie and Sylvie – almost like we're twins!"

"My Daddy calls me Shanny," the girl answered, tossing her blonde curls.

"Yes I do," Liam said, reaching past his wife to plant a kiss on his daughter's head. "Hello, sweetheart," he said to Anya, wrapping his arm around her shoulders. She stiffened.

"What a darling family," Sylvie said, beaming. "Good evening, Mrs. Leighton. Your husband does such wonderful work. Mr. Leighton," she said, giving a toss of her head. "We shall see you tomorrow."

"Eight o'clock sharp!" Liam said, giving a mock salute.

Mrs. Leighton waved her handkerchief and turned back over the hill, Anya glowering at her back.

Liam gave a happy sigh and sat down on the swing next to his daughter. He glanced up at Anya. "Good day, my love? You didn't feel like asking Mrs. Conorach to stay for a cup of tea?" he asked.

"I think we've seen quite enough of Mrs. Conorach for one day," Anya said, narrowing her eyes at her husband. "Whatever were you talking about so passionately on the walk back?"

"The stones, of course," Liam said. "She loves the stones I've been bringing over."

"Bringing over?"

"Yes, from the edge of our woodland. There are some wonderful, red-banded ones that we're using to frame her doorway."

"Our woodland?" Anya asked. "Do you mean you're giving away pieces of our land? Why would you do that?"

"Because they're paying for them, Anya!" Liam stood up now and walked to the other side of the porch, glancing out at the horizon. "Because I'm trying to provide for our family. And buy you lace, apparently, which I hear you are lacking."

"I never asked you for lace," Anya said. "What did Sylvie say to you?"

"She said you were planning to buy lace for that silk but that our funds were low."

"I never said – "

Liam put his hands up. "I'm tired, Anya. I had a good day. I thought *we* had a good day… and night. I don't know why we're arguing now."

"We're not arguing," said Anya.

"I'm not," Liam said, turning to go inside.

"Liam," Anya asked, trying to add a hint of bright playfulness that Sylvie Conorach had in her voice. The bright playfulness that used to be in her own voice, when the world was before her and Liam would look down at her with joy. "Mr. Doyle said there was a boat arriving at the pier this evening. Let's go meet it. Together."

Liam looked at her from the doorway. "I really am exhausted, Anya. But how about this: you go. Maybe ask Mrs. Conorach to go with you." Anya scoffed. "Or don't," Liam said. "But you should go if you'd like to go. You look like you need a break."

"And take the children? It will be too much with both of them alone."

"I'll stay with the tykes." He turned to Nellie who had been watching the conversation between her parents with eyes like saucers. "That'll be fun, Shanny-bun, won't it-?" The little girl nodded and burst into a grin. "It's settled then. Let's have supper and then you take a walk to the dock and see what new adventures embark from this ship."

"You won't fall asleep on the settee and leave them to their own devices?" Anya asked. Liam's face fell.

"For God's sake, Anya," he said quietly. "I'm doing everything I can here. I'm trying to help." He walked into the house and shut the door behind him.

CHAPTER FIFTY

The boat sailed through the glittering waters.
Anya was relieved to have made it to the shore of the
lake in time for what she called "the glistening." The time
of day before dusk where the sunlight made a golden,
glittering pathway from the horizon to the feet of any
person lucky enough to be standing on the shore. It was a
time when she felt she could breathe – be free. A time
when she could sense the beyond, sense the powers she
learned to harness so many years ago, the powers that
here in this woodland peninsula seemed so useless and
unneeded in comparison to her ability to scrub and cook
and change a dirty nappy.

The muscles in Anya's neck and shoulders relaxed
in the warm sunshine and an unbidden smile warmed
her face. She chatted with her fellow townspeople who
had come to greet the boat. As the boat carefully
navigated her way into the pier, Anya brought out a
clean, starched handkerchief and waved it in the air just
as her neighbors did. She smiled as people greeted
relatives and friends and others eagerly approached
boxes and crates, reading their labels and signing their X
on papers for receipt. The sailors ambled off, headed for

the pub, no doubt. The old sailing tunes burst into her brain, and she smiled at the memory. Finally, the happy commotion dwindled down and Anya glanced at her pocket watch on its silver chain. She should be heading back, but the sun had not fully set on the pier on this midsummer day. And Liam had said he would sit with the children. She fought with herself for a moment, and then decided she could stay just a bit longer. She walked down the shoreline, into the fading sunlight, her back to the ship. Anya was far away from the people now, and the tunes that floated in her head found their way to her throat. Quietly, she sang the Gaelic words to the rustling of the leaves on the trees. The flow of freedom began to seep through her veins. The sun in the west threw fire onto the water, the purples and pinks on the water to the east. For the first time in what felt like ages, she felt like herself. She felt like the person she was on the Island, the person she was as a young woman, the person she was when she met…

"Anya."

A voice from behind froze the blood in her veins.

CHAPTER FIFTY-ONE

"I would recognize that voice anywhere."

Anya knew that she needed to turn, propriety dictated that she needed to turn, meet his eyes, extend her hand, say something innocuous like 'good evening' or 'how where your travels' or 'was the weather satisfactory for the journey.' But her body was frozen, her voice mute. She swallowed hard as she sensed him take a step closer. Finally, she whispered so softly that the wind from the lake had to carry the word to his ears.

"Why?"

Cillian walked slowly around her, standing between Anya and the last of the day's sunlight. He waited several moments for her to look at him. She stared into the horizon, the only movement in her body a slight tremble in her lip. He reached out a hand to turn her chin to him and she instinctively slapped his arm away. "I'm sorry," he said, lowering his hand and adjusting his harp case on his shoulder.

It was the sight of the harp case that threw Anya back into consciousness. The harp that he played for her, the harp that had mesmerized her aunt, the harp that had coaxed notes out of her own body that she never knew were there, the harp that Hannah was bent over that awful night…

Fury, grief, longing, and a strange flaming sensation flew from below Anya's belly and into her head. She turned to him, eyes wet with tears and sparkling with feeling. "Sorry?" she asked. "For what?"

Now it was Cillian's turn to tremble. His deep chocolate eyes filled with tears as well, and he let a single drop fall down his cheek. He didn't raise a hand to wipe it away as he said, "For everything."

Anya swallowed hard several times, her limbs shaking, the palms of her hands damp. Cillian continued to look at her and she finally allowed herself to meet his eyes.

Everything.

Everything was in his eyes, in his lips, in the notes that sparkled in the air when he touched the instrument with his fingertips. And now everything was here. On her land. In her water. Floating on her air.

"Anya," he said again. She felt like she would collapse. "I'm sorry."

Anya cleared her throat to speak, to tell him that his apology for everything was everything, but it could fix nothing. Everything… was shattered.

"I'm sorry," he continued, straightening his shoulders. "I can see that I should call you Mrs. Something now."

"What?" she asked.

"Your jewelry," Cillian said.

"My jewelry… my jewelry shattered. Two winters ago. In the snow. It's lost…"

"Your ring," Cillian said, a tiny smile lifting the corner of his lips. Your wedding band, Anya. You're married."

Anya unconsciously covered her left hand with her right. "I am married," she managed to say. "To Liam. Liam Leighton."

"Well," Cillian said, reaching for her left hand and stroking her ring finger with the pad of his thumb. "That's as it should be… Mrs. Leighton." He released her hand gently. "Perhaps you could tell me where Uisean Hotel is? I'm to stay there until more permanent lodgings become available."

"It's over the hill there," Anya pointed. "Through that pathway."

"Is your home that way too?" Cillian asked. Anya nodded. "It's getting dark, Mrs. Leighton," Cillian said. "May I walk with you? At least until we're nearer to town?"

Anya looked at him full in the face. "You never seemed concerned with me walking in the dark before."

Cillian gazed at her, his eyes serious and sorrowful. "We were young then, Anya. And I was a fool."

CHAPTER FIFTY-TWO

The Saturday after the boat's arrival was the town fête to mark the first harvest of the corn, and the final harvest of the cherries. The transition from spring to autumn, from warmth and hope and life to the fullness of summer, bounty, and gratitude. It was time to ruefully accept the fading of the leaves on the trees, the very first harbinger of the cold desolate death of winter, while harvesting the best crops of the season. The town held a dance and auction each year, and everyone turned out in their Sunday best.

Anya had been distracted all week, burning bread, splashing dishwater all over the clean floor, even placing Isla in Nellie's bed for her nap, which caused the little girl enormous giggles and Nellie much indignation. A package had arrived on Thursday evening that was simply addressed to "The Lady of the House" with no return address. Inside was a piece of the finest lace Anya had ever touched. That night, Anya scorched the entirety of the dinner.

At first, Liam was amused by his pernicious wife's turn into flightiness, but when she ironed a burn mark on his best shirt, the amusement turned to frustration.

"I have to wear this to the Conorach's," he said. "We're meeting again to discuss the increase in cost of the wooden beams. He won't be happy, and I'll look foolish." Anya muttered an apology as she wrestled Isla to get her little dress over her head. "And," Liam said, following her through the main room "I have to wear it tonight."

"Just keep your jacket on," Anya said.

"You know it'll be boiling in there. All the other fellows will be in their shirts and suspenders." He sighed. "I guess I'll just have a pint or two to keep cool."

"Of course you will," Anya muttered, fastening the last button on the baby's dress.

"Anya, just leave it. The kids were sleeping before I rested my eyes."

"I believe you, but what I came home to after I saw... after I watched the boat launch... You were sound asleep with empty bottles of porter on the floor and the girls were playing in the larder!"

"No one was hurt," Liam almost shouted. Anya narrowed her eyes at him and pulled her shoulders back. "And I feel terrible about it. Terrible," he said softly. "I swear they had been sleeping."

Anya stood up and brushed invisible dust from her plum-colored skirt. Liam gave her a once-over. "Is that the dress you used to wear in Canada?" Anya nodded. "It's the one you wore that night in the pub, isn't it?"

Anya blushed and despite herself, smiled at her husband. "It is, Liam. It's my best one. That's why I chose it for tonight."

"Hmm," he said. "You should make yourself a new one, or rework that one. It's a bit out of step with what I see ladies wear in the village."

Anya's face fell. She had been working all week to forget Cillian, forget his presence here, forget that she may well see him tonight. Of course, forgetting was impossible, so she made her thoughts turned to how he abandoned her, how he betrayed her. She counted all the ways Liam was a kind husband, a loving father. Liam was light, and fun, and full of laughter, or he had been, a lifetime ago. These days, his laughter seemed to be reserved for other people – people who were brighter, better, had finer clothes.

She looked up into her husband's wide eyes. "I'm sorry to be a disappointment to you." Before he could see tears fall, she turned and marched up the stairs.

"I never said that," Liam called after her. He looked down at the little girl playing at his feet. "I only meant that she deserved something new," he said to the baby. "Something beautiful."

*   *   *

The dance hall, as predicted, was warm when they arrived. Liam took off his jacket and immediately joined his fellows, laughing as he made his way to the bar. Anya could hear him jovially taking the teasing he received about the burn mark in his shirt, and a spike of guilt pierced through her. It disappeared however, when she saw him grab a pint of dark beer and swallow half of it in one gulp. It was clear there would be no help for her tonight, and probably very little dancing. She took the children in hand and brought them to the church Sunday school teachers who had games set up and ice lollys. Anya chatted with the other mothers and tried to enjoy herself, but she longed to be dancing in Liam's arms.

A familiar sound floated through the air – the musicians were tuning up. People began to walk toward the barn for the dancing and Anya felt a presence behind her.

"Sing with me," he said, his breath warm on the back of her neck. She turned to him, aware of the women around her with their sharp ears and sharper tongues. "I've been asked to play and I'm a stranger here," he continued. "I need help."

"You have never needed help a day in your life," Anya whispered back.

"Well. As I told you on the pier, I was a kid and a fool. Now I know better. I know it takes brilliance beside you to make magic."

Anya looked around to see if Liam was watching this exchange. She caught sight of him, a head taller than most of the crowd, a pint in his hand. His second, or perhaps third. Beside him were Mr. Coronach, sitting with his back to the wall looking as if he was valiantly trying to follow the conversation. And Mrs. Coronach, her hair glittering in the fractured sunlight, slapping Liam lightly on the arm before exploding with laughter. Anya turned back to Cillian.

"I'll sing with you," she said.

"Thank you," Cillian said. "Thank you for everything."

Anya held his gaze. "I haven't done anything."

CHAPTER FIFTY-THREE

Hearing her sing… that voice rising up from such a slight, quiet woman - Liam had been transfixed. The woman on the pier, the woman clutching the pendant in the tea shop, the woman with her hand on Madeline's head, cooling her, that woman who walked to the altar towards him, stepped on a boat with him, held his arm as they walked onto unknown land, that woman who carried his children and birthed them with a bravery he would never comprehend. He had longed for this woman that he loved so fiercely. To remember her – to see her again – to hear her… it felt like a gift.

And Liam struggled to reconcile this woman, the woman he loved, with the woman that presently seemed to live in Anya's body and mind. The present woman was a tired woman, never content with all Liam had worked to give them, sad and frustrated in a way he couldn't understand. Or fix. How could both people exist in the same body? How could such a beautiful, talented, interesting woman ever be unhappy in this home he had built with the stones he had found? They might not be rich, but they had money enough for butter and thread, for meat and milk. And they had two healthy children. Anya worked hard of course, but he had found the stones and began his business, she no longer had to do back-breaking labor. What else could he do, could he give to her to bring out the woman he used to know – the woman who sang, who had embroidered beautiful silks and made jewelry like he had never seen?

Liam sipped his tea, which had gone cold. Anya had left the kitchen with a frown on her face. Again. He shook his head and swallowed his fears. There was nothing else he could do, he told himself. He was doing all that was expected of a man.

A shriek from the upstairs bedroom made him jump.

"What is it?" Liam called. "Is anyone hurt?"

"Oh no!" Anya moaned at the top of her voice. Liam took the stairs two at a time. He burst into the doorway of their bedroom and stared in shock.

And then he began to laugh.

Nellie and Isla sat in the corner of the room, covered in red lines that were too pink in color and too even to be blood. They also had pink powder in their hair and talcum footprints dotted the floor. Anya sat on the edge of the bed, clutching the bolt of yellow silk in her hands. She began to cry hot, angry tears.

"Anya, it's only lipstain and rouge," Liam said, trying to contain his laughter. "You can give them a good bath and it will come right off."

"No," Anya said between sobs. "Look at this!" She held out the silk, still crumpled in her hands. Liam stepped closer. Anya's fine embroidery flew across the edges. Lifting it, he could see that she had made the trees of their homeland sway in a breeze. Waves floated toward the middle of the blanket, and a small canoe of dark purple thread rode along them. Further down, he could see the beginnings of what looked like a ship, made of dark gray thread... the ship they had sailed on..."

"My God," he breathed. "It's unbelievable."

"I know," Anya wailed. "How could they have done this? I worked so hard!"

Done what?" Liam asked, following the shape of the boat with his finger. A streak of reddish pink peaked out of the crumpled fabric. He looked at his children, covered in lipstain.

"Mama drawed on the blanket," Nellie said, her eyes wide with guilt. "So we drawed on the blanket too."

Anya let the silk fall to the floor. Liam could see that on top of embroidered flowers and stones, houses and villages, the tykes had smeared the better part of Anya's brand new lipstain. And sprinkled it with most of the rouge and talcum powder she kept on the bureau. He looked at Anya.

"It's ruined," she said.

"Well..." Liam scratched his head. "Maybe you can get it out with soap and water?"

"It's lip*stain*, Liam," Anya said, ice in her tone. "It's mean to last."

"Well, if you work on it hard enough,"

"I worked on *this* hard enough," Anya cried. "I work on everything hard enough! I work, day and night, scrubbing floors, making meals you don't all don't even eat half the time, making clothes for you, cleaning them, ironing them."

"Well, you don't work too hard at ironing," Liam said with a twinkle in his eye, trying to get her to look at him from behind her tears. Trying to coax a smile.

Anya threw the fabric to the ground. "I tried to do one thing, make one thing that was mine – that was beautiful!" she shouted. The baby began to whimper.

Liam ran his hands through his hair. "I thought you were going to make it for us," was all he could think of to say.

"It was for us, it was…" Anya looked at their love story embroidered in the four colors of thread she could afford, weaving across the fabric. She had stayed up sewing until the moon was high in the sky for a week, sneaking out of the bedroom and by candlelight, humming the old tunes, trying to put all of her love, all of the good in her life that Liam had given her into this fabric so that she might remember what was right and true.

"It's gone," she whispered.

"It's just a blanket, Anya," Liam said.

"Just a blanket," she repeated, eyes narrowing to slits. "Of course you would say that."

Liam felt exhausted at all of this. Where had the girl from yesterday gone? Why was their home, which should be happy, always in such chaos? He was bothered by her sad moods, by her tears, by the mess, mostly because... he had no idea how to fix it. "If you had been minding the children" he said, the words tumbling out before he had a chance to think on them. "They wouldn't have had time to do all this."

Anya wanted to reach up and slap him.

Isla began to whimper in the corner. Anya stomped over, scooped her up and yanked Nellie up to a standing position. Without a word, she marched the children down the stairs.

CHAPTER FIFTY-FOUR

Orla Conorach spread the bolt of yellow silk on her kitchen table and gasped.

"I know," Liam said, wincing.

"Do you?" she asked, gently fingering the embroidery.

"It's so bad," he said.

"It's like a drawing, Mr. Leighton," Orla breathed. "Like a painting."

"Well, that's what Nellie said the tykes were doing," Liam said. "Drawing. But I don't think they should have."

Orla Conorach pulled herself up from staring at the embroidery and faced Liam. "Liam Leighton, as sweet as those children are, they should be horsewhipped for destroying work as fine as this. You're telling me that Anya made this?"

"Well, she was always good with embroidery," Liam said.

Orla scoffed. "Good at embroidery, you say?" She put her hands on her hips. "Mr. Leighton, your wife is an artist. I have never seen anything like this, not even in the best shops in the city. In fact, you should be horsewhipped yourself for not providing Anya with all the embroidery floss Mr. Doyle carries."

Liam's eyes widened and a proud smile spread across his face. "So you can fix it?" he asked.

"I can try," she said. "But lipstain is so called for a reason. It's a stain, Mr. Leighton." She laughed. "Why do you think so many men get in such trouble when their wives find a trace of pink or red on their collars? The evidence sticks." Liam's smile collapsed. "Oh don't look so downcast," she said. "The work that is unblemished can be cut out and sewn into something new eventually. Your best bet is to march yourself right down to Mr. Doyle's shop and buy Mrs. Leighton as much embroidery thread as you can. And," she looked sternly at him from under her blonde eyebrows. "A bouquet of flowers wouldn't go amiss."

"Yes ma'am," Liam said.

"Mr. Leighton," said Orla gently. "She's a good woman, your Anya. Quiet, maybe. But there's more to women than men see. Open your eyes."

*   *   *

A note had arrived on the porch after breakfast.
Dear Mrs. Leighton,

If you can spare the time, please bring your children and join me at the Smithy's shop at 2:00 pm. I would be interested to learn if you have any jewel that needs making or selling.

Respectfully,

C. Wallace

Anya could not spare the time. There was supper to be made, clothes to be laundered, and the children still showed streaks of red and pink from yesterday's escapades. The sunlight shone through the window and caught the white petal of a daisy Nellie had plucked from the yard. It almost sparkled. Anya swallowed hard. There wasn't time. There was never time. But today, she would make time. She plucked the kettle from the stove and filled it with water.

"Nellie," she called. "Get two towels. You children are getting one more bath. We're going out."

*   *   *

Anya carried Isla on her hip and Nellie ran ahead. The smithy had been wonderful and so welcoming. She had been able for the first time in years to work with the molten silver, tracing waves and swirls, sculpting ruffles. Cillian had been amazing with the children. At first, she didn't want to set them down or bring them near to him, but he brought from his bag two clever little drums, and an instrument with flat metal prongs fastened to a piece of wood. The children were enthralled and sat making ethereal tunes while she worked, and Cillian listened. The smithy had said she was welcome back any day, praising her work. Cillian had been a gentleman in every sense of the word, staying back, not reaching for her hand or looking too hard into her eyes. He had walked her and the children most of the way back home, the conversation focused on Nellie's continual questions about the trees and the birds, all of which Cillian answered patiently and in depth.

*   *   *

She stepped onto her porch feeling refreshed, lighter, and happier than she had felt in memory. Even the pain of the ruined blanket didn't sting as badly.

"The stew is burnt to a crisp," a voice called from inside. "Anya, what on earth did you do?" Liam's laughter broke her train of thought, and she heard the clatter of the lid.

"I thought if I set it over the coals while we were out, it would be ready for supper," Anya said, rushing to the hearth and lifting the lid. Black, brown, and rust-colored globs stuck to the pan.

"Clearly not," Liam said, still laughing. "And I'm famished. Where did you go all afternoon?"

"I didn't realize I was expected to ask for your permission," Anya said, trying to cover her guilt with indignation.

"I never said that," Liam said. "I was just making conversation – trying to make a joke. You hardly ever leave the house unless for errands. And you have never burnt the supper to sludge. So I thought there might be a story there – pardon me for asking," he said, slumping in the chair.

"I'll bake some quick bread for dinner and find something in the larder," Anya said, forcing a smile. "And we went to town. On a walk." She ducked her head into a cupboard. "Stopped by the smithy's."

"The smithy's?"

"Well, you know how I used to make jewelry. With my aunt, back in Canada." Anya made herself busy in the kitchen. "On the Island."

"Of course," Liam said. "I found your necklace, remember?" He smiled at her, but she wouldn't meet his eye.

"You did," Anya said, a smile creeping up on her face. She kept her head down, facing the stove. "Well, I wanted to see if perhaps I still had the talent for it."

"You have talent, Anya," Liam said. Something about the tone in his voice made her turn to him. She swallowed hard. "I saw Mrs. Conorach today," Liam continued. Anya turned back to the stove and began slamming pots down from the cupboard.

"Perhaps if you saw less of Mrs. Conorach, we might all be a little better off," Anya said. The final pot crashed onto the stove, rattling the china on the shelves.

"The Conorachs are my employers," Liam said. He was so tired of this conversation. Anya was a smart woman. Why did they continue to argue about this? "And Mrs. Conorach said you have talent. You make things that are beautiful."

"Not quite as beautiful and charming as her though," Anya said under her breath. Liam heard and sighed deeply. He went over to her.

"Anya," he said, touching her arm. "If you want to build something, you just have to do it. If you want to make something, whether it's embroidery, or silver jewelry, or whatever it is... Make it."

A tear fell into the dough Anya was kneading.

"I wanted to make us a better life," Liam said. "After that hard winter... I didn't ever want to see you like that again, out in the snow, trying to cook slop over the fire. And so I did. I found the stones and built this house, and built a business, Anya. For us." He squeezed her arm. "Everything I do, I do for us."

Anya turned to him. "I know," she said. "And everything I do, I do for us. And everything I don't do, everything, everything I've laid aside, I've laid aside because there's no time. There's no time left after I've done all the work I do for us."

"I've laid aside things too, Anya," Liam said. "My family, my friends, my career as an officer – don't you think I might have wanted to continue that? Rise in the ranks. But I couldn't stay there after…" It was Liam's turn to swallow hard. "It was best for me – for us, to leave. So I made that choice, abandoned that life."

"I know all that, and I'm grateful," Anya said. "I am. But Liam, here, now – you have friends, you have people you see every day."

"You could have friends too, if you tried," Liam said.

"When?" Anya asked. "When would I have time to see friends, even if I had them?"

"You have to make it, Anya," Liam said. "I can't figure this out for you. You have to make the time."

Anya looked away and nodded.

"You have to build your life just as I've built mine," he continued. "You have to make the time to make things, if that's what you want to do." Anya stared at the stove. She didn't see him pinch the bridge of his nose to wipe a tear away. She looked up as he cleared his throat. He looked at their children, dirty from their walk. He looked at the empty tea kettle and burnt stew on the smoldering hearth. He felt the weight of the bag of embroidery floss in his pocket. And he saw in his mind Caleb's bloody hat floating on the waves. Madeline's accusatory glare as her hand touched her swollen belly. He saw his wife as she was that winter day, gaunt and trembling in the icy wind. He saw his father's face watching them leave from the Canadian pier, stoney with disappointment. He saw the ruined bedspread his wife had made for him. And with a shake of his head, he gestured to the room and said out loud to himself, "But you have to make your things without making a mess of everything here."

"Understood," Anya said as the pain of his words encircled her heart.

CHAPTER FIFTY-FIVE

In the weeks after, Anya let the dust settle on the windowsills and made simple suppers. Once a week on Thursdays, she took the children with her to the smithy. Sometimes Cillian would meet her, sometimes not. He would always leave a note on her porch around midday on the day she was scheduled to visit the smithy to let her know whether he would be there or not. On the days he came, they would talk about music and the old days back home while the silver was cooling. The second time they met, she had forced herself to inquire about Hannah. Cillian's face got dark as he told her in a choked voice that Hannah had died in childbirth. The child, he said, had died too. Anya expected to feel the sweet relief of revenge. Instead, she felt nothing but pity.

It was a bright Thursday morning and Anya dressed with extra care. She pulled the wooden box out of her bureau and took the key from her bedside table. Placing Cillian's latest note inside, she reached in and took out what remained of her lipstain. She applied the smallest amount and smudged her lips together. Her eyes were clear and her hair shone from the extra brushing she had given it last night. She smiled despite herself and put the key back in the bedside table.

"Come, children," she called. "Time for the Smithy! Mr. Wallace has written that he has a special surprise in store for us today."

"Yea yea yea!" Nellie said, lifting Isla into her wagon.

"Put the basket in with her, Nellie. That's a good girl." After Cillian had told her about Hannah's death and the death of the baby, she always made a point to bring him a fresh loaf of bread and whatever produce was fresh from her garden.

Liam seemed unconcerned with her meeting Cillian occasionally at the Smithy's. Anya had described him as an old friend she knew from her hometown. Liam had asked a few brief questions about Cillian's appearance here of all places, and Anya told Liam what Cillian had told her: he was here to revive the music program at the church. Liam had shrugged and said with a laugh that as long as he wasn't served ashes for dinner and the children were minded, it was fine with him if she chatted with a childhood friend while she worked at the Smithy.

"Mr. Bulance is home sick today," Cillian said, greeting them at the door. "It seems he ate a bad piece of fish for dinner last night."

"Oh no," Anya said. "And I had so hoped to try my hand at making a pendant."

"I know you did," Cillian said. "That's why I happened to call on him with some packets of ginger tea and asked if he could leave the fire going. Happily for us, he obliged."

"Cillian - Mr. Wallace, that was so kind of you," Anya said, a heat rising in her chest. "But I worry it's not proper: you and I here without Mr. Bulance."

"Oh Anya, it's the middle of the day. And your children are here. If you're really not comfortable, I'm happy to leave. Although, it would be a good idea for someone to be watching the children while you work with molten hot metal." He smiled, that old smile that clenched her heart. "I'll do whatever you decide," Cillian said, "But first, I brought a surprise." He stepped toward them and ruffled both children on the head. "Now make sure to make a big mess on your clothes with these lollys, little ones. We want Mama to have something to do in the evenings while your Papa rests from a hard day at work."

Anya blushed. Talking to Cillian had become so easy and free, she supposed she had let slip too many details of their chaste and tired evenings at home.

"And for Mother," Cillian said. Walking up to Anya and offering a package wrapped in lace. "Be very careful, Anya," he said. She could smell his aftershave and the commercial starch on his jacket. "These are precious."

He took her hand with one of his and pressed the package into her palm. With shaking fingers, Anya pulled back the folds of lace to reveal three sparkling stones. An opal, screaming with pink and teal fire, an emerald-cut garnet, red as blood, a pear-shaped topaz as blue as the spring sky.

"My request is this," Cillian said. "If you can make pendants for each of these; your own design, I can sell them. I will give you half the profits. And," he said, placing his hand on Anya's arm. "You will choose one for yourself. To keep." He stepped closer and she could smell mint and herbs on his breath.

"You once offered me a choice, Anya," he said. "I chose the wrong thing. The false thing. Now I give you a choice. A chance to choose beauty. A beauty of your own."

"Mama mama!" a little voice called from the wagon. Anya closed her hand around the stones and tore her gaze from Cillian.

"Yes, precious?" she asked, bending to the little girl.

"She dropped her lolly," Nellie said. "Now it's dirty."

Anya picked up the lolly from the floor and tried to blow the sand off it. Cillian stepped over and a with a wink to Nellie, he took the lolly from Anya's hand and popped it in his mouth, wincing at the grit of the dirt. When he handed it back to the baby, it was shiny. "A little dirt won't always hurt you," he said.

"Now," Cillian said, smoothing his trousers. "We must let your mother get on with her art. I'll stay with you and play drums for a bit, shall I? And let's go into the yard under the trees. Anya, do you approve?"

She nodded, words stuck in her throat.

"Yes then? Alright, little ones. Let's go." Cillian stood up and gestured for Nellie to pull the wagon outside. Turning back to Anya, he raised her free hand to his lips and kissed it.

"Anya," he said. "You always have a choice."

CHAPTER FIFTY-SIX

The Harvest Festival. Mugs of cider, some laced with a bit of the spirit, to welcome the spirits. People who lived in this isolated place, who made their homes and their lives in harmony with the land, the water, and the air always took the time to give respect to the Source of Life. They went to the churches each Sunday, of course, but a nod, a flower, and homage or a prayer was always offered to the Great Spirit, who, it was quietly understood, could not be ensconced in the confines of liturgy and rhetoric.

The summer had faded into autumn with a placidity that prickled. There was a fragile peace in the Leighton household. Anya made time to go to the Smithy's each week, and they didn't speak of the ruined silk piece. Anya assumed Liam had put it in the dustbin.

As the Festival approached, Anya had suggested that Liam that he take his fiddle down from the rafters to tune it, to play with the musicians of the town. After much laughing refusal, she undertook the task herself. When she opened the case, she found the instrument unrecognizable; the wood warped and cracked, the strings broken and curled. Liam had taken one glance at it and slammed the case shut.

"I wished you would have listened to me," he had said. "It's broken – ruined. You might as well use it for firewood." Walking past the iceboxes with its bottles of porter, he went straight to the top cupboard and pulled down the bottle of moonshine, filling a clay mug almost to the top. "I swore never to play again after…" He looked hard at Anya. "After he died."

*   *   *

The full moon began to peek over the horizon as the children of the village dozed on haybales inside the church. Mothers covered the children with blankets they had brought from home. Anya began singing the lullaby that coaxed Nellie and Isla to sleep each night, and other women watched with kind eyes as their children scooted a little closer to Mrs. Leighton.

Little eyes closed and little hands held blankets closer to their chests, some children nuzzling up to the stuffed toys they had brought.

"I think they're done for," Mrs. Walsh, a fellow mother from Sunday School said, squeezing Anya's shoulder gently. "They won't wake again until they find themselves in their beds tomorrow morning. It's time for us to have a few hours of fun." Anya smiled at her, worry still evident behind her eyes. "Auntie Teresa is here to watch over them," she said. A vision of Aunt Airmed suddenly appeared in front of Anya, floating in a violet gown.

Your children will be cared for, a voice seemed to say, echoing throughout the room. Mrs. Walsh stared at Anya's stricken face and gave her shoulder another squeeze. "Auntie Teresa may be older than Moses, but she's reliable. Come on, let's find Mr. Leighton. You need a warm drink and a dance." She pulled Anya to her feet and led her outside.

The two ladies walked into the cool night and surveyed the festivities. "Well," Mrs. Walsh said with a rueful smile. "I see Mr. Leighton." Anya glanced where she was looking and there was her husband, sitting on a haybale gazing up at Orla Coronach, by all counts deep in conversation. "Let's go say hello, shall we?" Mrs. Walsh said. "Orla runs her mouth far too quickly; it's about time someone else had a word in." She began to lead Anya over, but Anya pulled her arm away.

"No," Anya said. "Let them chat. It's the most animated I've seen Liam in weeks." She forced a smile. "I believe I'll take a constitutional. If you'll excuse me."

"Oh Anya," Mrs. Walsh said. "Have a backbone. Go get what belongs to you."

Anya smiled. "I have as much backbone as most people you've met, Mrs. Walsh. It's just a bit more…

hidden." She patted the other woman's arm and turned to walk toward the edge of the woodland.

The tight chignon at the nape of her neck was beginning to give her headache. She had shoved the pins in rather forcefully that evening after the argument over the fiddle, and now they felt like they were piercing her scalp. Anya stepped into the glade of moonlight in the woods. Pulling the pins out gently, she felt the tightness of the chignon fall into loose waves that tumbled down her back. The tension behind her eyes subdued a bit. It wasn't proper for her to return to the festival with her hair loose and down, but she couldn't bear to pull it back tightly. Not just yet. She lowered herself onto a log and smoothed her skirts out. Anya raised her face to the moonlight. Placing the hairpins in her pocket, her fingers brushed a lace-wrapped package. She pulled it out and unfolded the lace.

"So, have you made a choice?" he asked.

CHAPTER FIFTY-SEVEN

The jewels glowed in the moonlight.

Cillian knelt in the moss at her feet. He took her hand in his and closed her fingers over the stones. Anya began to shiver.

"Here," Cillian said, shaking off his peacoat and wrapping it around her shoulders. "And here." From the ground behind him, he produced two mugs and handed one to her. "A warm drink will do you good."

She shook her head. "I'm not drinking. Not liquor. Someone has to take care of my children."

"Well, I can understand that," Cillian said, setting both mugs gently on the forest floor. "From the looks of it, Mr. Leighton has had no problem putting back several pints. I don't think he'll be much help taking care of Nellie and Isla." He sat back on his heels and gazed up at her. "And Anya, someone needs to take care of you."

"I can take care of myself," she said, pushing Cillian's coat off her shoulders. He rose to stop her, pulling the coat around her neck and holding it at by the lapels.

"Anya, stop," he said gently. "It's only a coat. And this is only tea." He proffered the mug again. She reached for it and raised it to her nose. She could not smell a trace of alcohol, just a blend of herbs.

"Cillian, wherever did you get this tea?" she asked. "They're only serving cider."

"I asked the matron to boil some water. And I brought the tea. I always carry some with me these days."

"I thought you always carried your harp with you," Anya said, taking a careful sip from the mug. The tea tasted of chamomile, lavender, and something else... something earthy and sweet.

"I used to," Cillian said. "Not anymore."

"Does no one play music anymore?" Anya asked quietly.

"You do," Cillian said. He rose and sat next to her on the log. "I heard you. In the church. Singing that lullaby."

The warmth of his body next to hers sent shivers up her spine. "How could you possibly know it was me?" she asked.

"How could you possibly think I could forget the sound of your voice?" Cillian brushed his fingers over her hand. Anya moved away.

"You forgot it easily enough all those years ago." Anya knew she shouldn't speak of a man's dead wife, shouldn't bring up his pain, but even after a decade, hers was still as fresh as the dew that would gather in this very forest in a few short hours.

Cillian sighed. "I forgot everything, Anya," he said. He was a quiet as she'd ever heard him. "I forgot the promises I made to you; I forgot my temper. I forgot that I had to work hard and not just hope for good luck if we were to build a life together." He turned to her, but did not reach for her. "I wanted so badly to make our lives beautiful that I forgot what beauty really is."

Anya lifted her chin. She was seduced by his words all that time ago, by his poetry, by his music. Seduced by her aunt and the magic and the Island. But she had discovered that life could not be sustained by music and words and ways of the old days. Life was pain. Life was guilt and love and jealousy. Life was hard, back-breaking work if you hoped to keep one ounce of the joy or beauty you tried so hard to create. She held his gaze in her fierce one. "What is beauty?" she asked.

"Beauty is patience," Cillian said plainly. "Beauty is love. A love that lasts… through time, through distances. Beauty is forgiveness."

Anya felt her mouth grow dry. There were no words she could find to answer him. Cillian looked at her, looked through her, he seemed to bore into her very soul. But he did not touch her.

"Drink your tea," he said, in a voice as soft and tender as the first petals of spring. She held his gaze, heart racing, as she lifted the mug to her lips and drained its contents. He took the cup from her hand, brushing her fingers with his. "Walk me," he said. "Warm yourself." Cillian rose to his feet and offered his arm. Standing in the moonlight, she felt a million stars fly through her veins, a shifting and a sparkle she had only ever felt twice before. Once, in a cabin in the woods with the music of a harp hanging in the air, and once again when she had seen the Great Spirit stand over her the day her mother left this world. She felt that otherworldly feeling now. And she felt tired, so very tired.

"Lean on me," Cillian said. Her feet felt as if they were floating in her shoes, and she found she was too exhausted to protest. They walked into the woodland, along the pathway to the lighthouse. The sounds of the festival disappeared behind them. Soon, the splashing of the waves and the crunch of the leaves beneath their feet were all that could be heard.

"Cillian, we can't walk too far," Anya said, out of breath. "My children are still at the festival."

"Your children will be taken care of," he said in a voice that sounded like an echo in her ears – an echo she had heard somewhere before. She swayed on her feet. Why was she so tired? Despite herself, she leaned her head against his shirt, the linen smelt fresh, and the skin beneath warmed her cheek.

"Let's rest," he said. Stepping in front of her, he took both of her hands in his and led them into a grove of trees. "A fairy circle," he said, smiling at her. "Perfect for magic."

Anya put her hand to her forehead, which was beginning to pound. She felt a strange lightness in her veins and the exhaustion was overwhelming her.

"Sit with me," Cillian said, leaning against a tree and pulling her back against his chest. He bent his face into her hair and inhaled her scent, he heard her sigh and relax against him. A groan escaped his lips. He dared to kiss her hair, and when she didn't protest, he brushed the waves aside and laid a gentle kiss on her neck. She shuddered and began to breathe quickly.

"Anya," Cillian whispered, taking her shoulders and adjusting her so he knelt in front of her, looking into her cloudy eyes. He lifted her chin.

"I'm so tired," she said, swaying in his grip.

"This will make you feel alive," he answered. He leaned forward and kissed her neck, felt her shudder. "More alive than you have felt in a long time." He leaned back to look at her, her eyes clouded and her body shivering. "As I told you before, Anya," he said, gripping her arms tightly. "You have a choice. You have always had a choice."

"I…" she said, swaying toward him, her eyes closing. He caught her, the back of her head in the palm of his hand, wrapping his other arm around her waist. Holding her, he leaned forward and kissed her. First, brushing his lips to hers, tasting their softness and then pushing her mouth open, kissing her harder. He pulled her toward him and felt her hands tighten around his arms. With great effort, he pulled himself back and looked at her face. Her eyes were closed, her face was pale. Her breath was coming in shallow bursts. Holding her head firmly in his hand so it did not droop, he leaned forward and whispered in her ear.

"What is your choice?"

Anya was dizzy, sinking, she needed help. She needed him to help her stand, to go back, to splash water on her face. She needed to ask him for help. She opened her eyes and tried to tell him, tried to scream at him for help. In a whisper, all she could say was "Cillian…"

A smile spread across his face, and he laid her back in the dry leaves and covered her body with his own.

CHAPTER FIFTY-EIGHT

Liam had begun to panic in earnest. Orla Conorach had taken his children to sleep at her house for the night. A search party was being organized. "I'm sure we don't need all that," he said to Colm Conorach. "Right?"

"Liam, I hate to say this, but there have been bears sighted in these woods. And we know there are wolves." Colm coughed uncomfortably. "And," he continued, wringing his hands together and looking out at the edge of the forest. "They're saying that Cillian Wallace... Well, they're ordering a search party for him too."

"Cillian's missing?" Liam asked. The cold wind seemed to sink right into his bones. Anya spends most Thursdays with him at the Smithy's.

"I know," Colm said quietly.

"Well, if she's with him, I'm sure he's keeping her safe."

Colm patted Liam's arm. "Let's hope that's the case," he said.

Liam, along with most of the men in the town, searched the woods as the full moon rose high in the sky. A great howling was heard throughout the forest and at each wail, Liam felt that his heart had been pierced by something eternal. He had lost his best friend, lost Madeline, lost his parents. He could not lose Anya. She was all he had, she had given him a family, a life. How could he have let this happen?

"Anya!!" Liam called for what seemed like the hundredth time, his voice hoarse with effort. Only the howl of wolves answered him back.

The morning dawned, overcast and chill. Liam sat with his head in his hands, the coffee the Rector's wife had set before him cooling in its china cup. He looked up when he heard Colm Conorach's footsteps in the hall.

The hope in Liam's eyes nearly broke Colm's composure. He found he could not speak just yet, so he merely shook his head. The light in Liam's eyes went dim and he placed his head back in his hands.

A noise was heard in the hall, a noise that the two men quickly began to identify as running footsteps. "We found something," Timothy said. "By the beach." Timothy held up a scrap of plum silk. Liam jumped up and snatched it out of his hand.

"Oh my God," Liam said, tears swelling behind his eyes. "It's… this is her dress." He grabbed Timothy. "Where did you find this? Take me there now – please!"

Colm Conorach snatched up their jackets and they raced after Timothy. The wind whistled and screamed in their uncovered ears as all three men ran at full speed in the direction of the beach. It was quicker to go through the meadow than the woods, and they raced until their hearts felt like bursting.

"Where did you find it?" Liam asked once Timothy stopped. "Show me – please – where?"

"Here!" a voice yelled, hoarse and straining. All three men looked to the south. "Here! Please help me, please! I'm injured!"

"It's not her," Liam said, staring at Colm before taking off in the direction of the sound. "Keep shouting, man, so we can find you!" Liam yelled between breaths. Within moments, they had found him, tucked into a pile of driftwood, coatless and bleeding.

"I'm sorry, I'm sorry," Cillian said, his voice shaking. The men lifted him up and Colm looked at the seeping wounds to his shoulder and thighs.

"Tell us what happened," Mr. Conorach said, trying to mask the fury in his voice.

"Wolves," Cillian said, gripping what looked like one broken arm with another. "Wolves…"

"Where is Anya?" Liam asked, ducking down to meet the man's eyes.

"I," Cillian stammered, shivering still. "I don't…"

Liam saw the lie on his dirt-covered face and grabbed him hard by the arms. "Where is Anya?" he shouted, shaking Cillian. "Where the hell is my wife?"

"Liam, he's probably going into shock," Colm said, placing a hand on Liam's flexed arm. "We need to get him back and warmed up before he can tell us anything useful."

"Damn that to hell," Liam said, still staring at Cillian. "Where is my wife?" Liam's voice was deathly low. Then, with a sudden growling shout, Liam gave him another fierce shake. Three shining objects fell out of Cillian's shirt and into the sand. With one hand still grasping Cillian, he bent and picked them up. Immediately he recognized the swirls and eddies, the same patterns Anya had woven into the yellow silk blanket, the same decoration on the pendant he had found and had been lost again, so long ago. "These are Anya's," Liam whispered.

"Those are mine," Cillian shot back, spitting blood on the ground and shaking.

In one swift movement, Liam pocketed the stones and drew back his arm, delivering a hard blow to Cillian's cheek. Cillian fell to the ground and Liam, much bigger, much taller, fell on top of him, landing a blow with each word. "You. Know. Where. She. Is! Tell. Me. Now!" It took both the other men to pull Liam off. Mr. Conorach took Liam by the arms and swung him around. "Goddammit Liam, get ahold of yourself! This bastard knows where she is, you know it and so do we. He'll have to tell us. But if you kill him, he won't be able to talk."

The blood vessels in Liam's nect pulsed and his eyes were as wide as saucers in fury. "I'll tear him apart," he growled.

"And I'll help you," Mr. Conorach said. "But after he tells us where to find Anya."

CHAPTER FIFTY-NINE

Cillian woke up on a hard bench, every bone in his body pounding. One eye was swollen shut but he could see tall vertical lines blurring and swaying in and out of his vision.

"Oh good, you're up," a voice said in the distance. "Dirty bastard."

Cillian found his own voice. "That man… Leighton… he attacked me."

"And well you deserved it most likely."

"You have to catch him – throw him in jail."

"Well, we've only the one cell in here," said the sheriff. "And I don't think you'd like me to make Liam Leighton your neighbor just now. He'd rip you to shreds as fast as you could say Jack Robinson."

Cillian could just make out a man standing up and bringing something near the blurring lines. He stood and stumbled toward him.

"Have a drink," the sheriff said, splashing a bucket of cold water on Cillian who sputtered and threw his hands forward, finding the bars of the cell and gripping them. "That should wake you right up," the sheriff said fiercely. "And loosen your tongue."

The sheriff swung open the door and handcuffed Cillian, dragging him into a room and plunking him down on a wooden chair. "Now then you whining bastard. Tell me where we can find Mrs. Leighton."

"I don't know anything," Cillian said, reaching up to wipe the spittle and blood from his face where the water had washed it down.

"We found her jewelry in your pocket," the sheriff said. "We found a scrap of her dress near the beach where we found your sorry self."

"She gave it to me," Cillian said, staring at the wall behind the sheriff.

"If I were a betting man, I'd say you took it," the sheriff said, standing and leaning over Cillian who glowered but crouched back in his chair. "And I'll tell you something else you piece of shit. We found a piece of her dress tucked into your sleeve."

Cillian winced as he heard a door slam and the unmistakable shout of Liam Leighton's voice in the next room.

"Sounds like Anya's husband out there if I'm not mistaken," the sheriff said. "Liam doesn't know about the torn dress in your sleeve yet. If you don't have any more information for me as to Mrs. Leighton's whereabouts, I'll step out and tell him and let *him* finish the questioning."

Cillian swallowed hard as the sheriff placed the torn fabric on the table. "I'll give you until the time I count ten," the sheriff said. "One, two, three…"

"Let me see him," Liam shouted. "She could have frozen to death by now, we're wasting time!"

"Five, six, seven," the sheriff continued.

"… and if I find her hurt, I will tear him limb from limb!"

"Nine…" The sheriff turned to unlock the door.

"She's," Cillian muttered.

The sheriff turned, keys jangling in his hand. "Yes?"

"The wolves," Cillian said. "I can tell you everything, but you have to promise if you find her to let me out on the next boat."

"Tell me, you thieving bastard," the sheriff said. "Or I let him in NOW."

Cillian let out a shuddering breath. "The wolves took her. They came at us and took her. She was unconscious…"

"Unconscious? Did they attack her?"

Cillian stumbled for words. "She was tired… exhausted during our walk, so I laid her down…"

"You *what?*" The sheriff slammed a fist on the table.

Cillian glared at him now. There was no need to hide the truth. True, the tea might have had herbs in it that made things easier, but she had said his name…

"I laid her down." Cillian said calmly, a smirk making its way across his broken face. "She was nearly asleep. But as I lay beside her, the wolves came."

"And they attacked her?"

"They attacked me!" Cillian said, shouting now. "As you see. And I will have my lawyer on you for throwing me in jail for no crime and refusing me a doctor's care. And for false accusation."

"WHERE THE HELL IS ANYA LEIGHTON?" the sheriff shouted

Pounding fists sounded on the door.

Cillian stared at the sheriff. "I tried to fight them off. Off both of us. I ran into the woods to find a stick, anything to beat them off. But when I came back, I could see... the wolves had dragged her away."

"You absolute bastard," the sheriff said. "You'll help us find her – lead us to where they are. And when you're done, you'll go right back to jail. For the crime of abandonment." He took an envelope from his jacket and threw it on the table. "A letter. From one Hannah Leighton. Your wife." Cillian went pale. "Who, as is evidenced by her writing, you have abandoned in Canada," the sheriff continued. "Along with your child."

CHAPTER SIXTY

Two figures stood before her limp frame. Darkness held the cave in its embrace and the dirt floor smelt of centuries of life, and death.

"The circle to which we belong." Dark gray hair floated above Anya's waist and brushed her cheek. "What have we done to her that she ended up here?"

The second figure brushed up against Anya's hand. "It wasn't what we did." The voice was like a flute on the wind. "It was what we failed to do."

"We must keep her warm."

"Can we not…"

"No, sister. We cannot. She must stay here." The first gray figure curled up beside Anya on the cold ground. She brought glowing eyes up to the white figure who followed suit and curled up on the other side so that Anya lay warm between them.

*   *   *

Anya saw in her dreams colors of a kaleidoscope, puce green and fuchsia, great skirts circling and dancing, surrounding her, choking her. She fought against it, against it all, but she couldn't break through. The songs her mother sang swirled around her mind on a broken violin, scratched and tuneless. The words were jumbled, neither English nor Gaelic.

Suddenly, she was in her canoe, floating across the waves to the Island. Her mother swam beside, disappearing under the waves and jumping from them to become a bird in the sky.

She was at the Island. Airmed stood on the rocky beach, wrinkles gone, hair black as a raven.

"Eilidh." Airmed held out her hand. Anya found herself beside her Aunt once more, the stone smooth under her feet. "You cannot be like me. I gave myself to the Spirit, to the stones, to the songs, to the magic. I could have helped the whole village; I wanted to. But they did not want to hear. Perhaps I did not have the words to tell them."

Airmed passed Anya to her mother who seemed to float on the air.

"My daughter."

She embraced Anya who inhaled her mother's scent of lavender and rose. There was another scent in her mother's hair, something westerly... the scent of absolution. In a wrenching moment, her mother was floating just out of her reach. "We cannot break the veil,"

Liora said gently. "I must tell you, before it is over. I gave myself to the world, Anya. I hid the magic, the songs, the stones. I wanted to give the world what the world wanted of me."

"And it killed you," Anya said. "Aren't you angry?"

"Oh Anya," her mother said, smiling down at her. Anya could feel her mother's soft hand on her cheek even as she stood so far away. "There is no anger here. No sadness. No grief. There is only peace. And the joy of watching you."

"But what the world wanted of you – it killed you. I gave the world what you wanted to give – two children. And yet there is still anger here, and sadness – so much sadness. Why?"

Liora shook her head. "I may have failed the world, with its impossible expectations. But I gave the Spirit what She wanted of me. I gave her you."

"What does She want of *me*?" Anya whispered, stepping toward her mother. Liora's white skirt turned to mist as Anya came closer.

"Bravery," Airmed said, now floating next to Liora. "Beauty. Patience. Love. That is what we see in you."

"You have given these to the world," Liora said, floating in and out of the gathering mist. "Now you must give them to the Spirit. You must trust the Spirit."

"Don't go, please-" Anya whispered. "What does that mean? I don't know how... Mama..."

"The Spirit is you and You are Her," Liora said, her shape dissolving into the mist. "And we ride on the wind. Always."

Anya reached out for her mother, stepped toward where she had been. She felt a swirl of warmth around her, lifting her hair, brushing a whisper of love onto her forehead.

"You must not go alone," Airmed said. Anya turned to see her aunt. Airmed looked as true and solid as Anya remembered her. "You must not go alone like I did," Airmed said. "I wanted solitude. I was made for it. You, though…" Airmed smiled at Anya. "There is one who was made for you, and you for him. He loves you. You have a village who needs you. You have children." The women stared at each other. "Children with your mother's eyes. You must teach them. You must teach them all."

"My children," Anya whispered.

"Your children have their mother's heart."

"Anya!" a voice wailed in the air. Airmed lifted her hands to gather the wind around her and then she pushed it away. "She is strong, Liora. She is brave. We must go through." Airmed turned to Anya and placed a palm on her forehead.

"Sleep," she commanded.

Anya's world went black.

CHAPTER SIXTY-ONE

Sunlight flickered through the curtains and brushed Anya's cheek. Her eyes fluttered open. The air in the room was golden and soft. Her hand grasped the coverlet and her eyes came into focus.

The silk.

Trying to return to the world, Anya traced the stitches. Water. Trees. Children. Stones, Wind, swirling through the flower petals, through leaves, through everything. Her life, set in golden sunlight. She glanced farther on, there was no stain to be found.

A light knock on the door. Liam entered. At the sight of his face, Anya remembered all that had passed in the forest, all that she had felt the last few months. A knifelike pain gripped her heart.

With a step, Liam was at her side.

"You're back," he said. His rough hand reached up and brushed a hair from her forehead.

"I..." Anya said, her voice a hoarse whisper.

"Shh," Liam said. Rest. You need rest, the doctor said."

"Liam, I need to tell you-"

"No, Anya." Liam bent down to kiss the top of her hair, as gently as the kiss of the summer wind. He rested his forehead on the crown of her head. When he rose again, there was something deep in his eyes that Anya had not seen in years. He took a breath and looked at her. Finally, he took both her hands in his. "You don't need to tell me anything, Anya. I know."

She wanted to pull her hands away in shame, but felt she was gripping his. "I'm sorry, Liam." She began to weep. "I'm sorry."

"You will not be sorry," Liam said, his voice choked. "You have nothing to be sorry for." He bent toward her and wiped the tears from her cheeks with his thumb. "Anya, he poisoned you."

"I know," she said between sobs. "With his words, with his... promises."

"Anya, look at me. Please." Liam stroked her hair until she could breathe calmly enough to stop her tears. She raised her eyes to his. "Cillian poisoned you with herbs. In the tea. He brewed salvia and kratom, enough to make a horse sleep for days." Liam's jaw worked and he stared out the window for a moment to push the sheriff's words out of his mind so he could speak calmly. Finally, he turned to her. "But he didn't..." Liam stopped, unable to repeat the words the doctor had told him. They were not enough. "I know he hurt you, but he..."

"The wolves," Anya breathed. Liam stared at her.

"You remember?" he asked.

"I tried to tell Cillian to stop, to find help," she said, words tumbling out. "But I couldn't speak, I couldn't... I was sinking. And then there was the fiercest sound... so fierce and full of fury. There were two..." she shook her head, her eyes blurry, and she didn't see the tears running down her husband's face. "They fell on him, tearing at his skin, his clothes. He struck out at them, hitting and kicking. Finally I saw him run... Deep into the woods. The white wolf began to race after him, but the gray called her back. They came back, encircled me. I could see their eyes. So blue. Blue like the sky on a winter's morning. And then..." Anya shook her head, trying to remember. "I was flying... no... floating. And tired. And suddenly so warm. And then I dreamed..." She blinked hard, seeing the dream as clear as the day dawning in the window. Seeing as clearly as Liam's pale face, the deep shadows under his wide eyes. The wetness on his skin. She reached a hand up and cupped his cheek. He shut his eyes and leaned into her palm.

A warmth filled her heart, wrapped itself around it, settling.

"I didn't see you, Anya," Liam whispered. "I did, once. But I haven't seen you, really, in so long. I'm sorry."

"If I can't apologize, neither can you," Anya said, smiling at him.

"Yoo hoo!" A bright voice echoed up the stairs. "Neighborly Nurse Service calling! Anya's face tightened, and then she heard the sound of her children laughing.

"Are they?" Anya breathed, fear in her eyes.

278

"Perfectly fine," Liam said. "Missing their mother, but Doctor said no visitors without his approval."

"Mr. Leighton?" the voice said quietly, at the door now. The handle turned and Orla Conorach stepped over the threshold, her face full of concern, and then, seeing Anya awake, breaking into outright joy. "Oh my dear," she said, her voice low and soft. "The look of you."

"I must be a fright," Anya said.

"No no, I'm so very sorry to have disturbed, but to see you. To see you awake." Orla bit her lip. "You are my friend, Anya. And I... I want to help. Help you. I've brought fresh bread, and broth. I should have brought something for the whole family, I'm sorry, but... I had hoped..."

"You had hoped?" Anya asked.

"I had hoped so much that you would be well enough to eat something."

Anya looked at her, this woman, this neighbor, this friend, that she hadn't understood until now. That she hadn't seen.

Orla wrung her hands in the doorway, looking at Anya and trying valiantly to stop herself from bustling over to the bedside. She could see that Anya's husband was doing all the care that needed to be done. In a voice too bright for the room, she asked, "Do you like the coverlet?"

Anya wrinkled her brow in confusion.

"The stain is gone," Orla said quickly. "Mr. Leighton brought it to me weeks ago and I tried a little of this, a little of that. Nothing would lift that blasted stain. And the night... the night you were attacked..." Orla swallowed hard before continuing. "Mr. Leighton carried Nellie and Isla to my house. He was so distraught that Colm offered him a drink of... Well, I'm afraid to say it was moonshine. He refused, did Mr. Leighton, knocking the bottle over onto the table in his haste to leave. To find you. The moonshine spilled all over the coverlet, soaking it. And once the children were comfortable in bed, well, I couldn't sleep for worrying. And so I scrubbed and scrubbed and before the sun rose in the sky, the stain lifted away with it. I..." Orla stopped, flustered.

Anya lifted her head and looked at the blanket, the entirety of which was a golden as the ring on her finger. Breathless, she lay her head back on the pillow and turned to Orla.

"Thank you," she said. Her voice was warm as she held the other woman's gaze.

"No no, it was no trouble. I would do anything I could to help you. But now I see you must rest. I've intruded..."

"Mrs. Conorach, you are welcome in our home anytime," Anya said. "And I need to see my children, I don't need to rest." She began to lift herself to climb out of bed.

"My love, you do," Liam said, placing a gentle hand on her shoulder. "Please. Please stay there. I'll bring the tykes to you." Anya nodded and lay back. Liam bent down to kiss her forehead before leaving the room. Orla looked at Anya, seeing the bags under eyes.

"I'll be getting on my way," she said. "I'm sorry to disturb, Mrs. Leighton."

"Could you stay a moment, Orla?" Anya patted the bedside. "I want to ask you a question."

Orla walked over to the bed and sat gingerly down, spreading her skirts. "Mrs. Leighton, I never... I'm very sorry if you ever had the impression that I was keeping Mr. Leighton for any purpose other than business – " Anya brushed her words away.

"I know," Anya said quietly. "Well, I know now. That's not my question. My question is... well... a question that you don't ask of husbands."

"Mrs. Leighton, I wouldn't have the first idea..."

"You were in the room when the doctor came, Orla," Anya said, squeezing her hand. "I don't remember everything, but I remember you. You were holding my children. Keeping them safe."

Orla nodded. "I did try," she said.

"You kept my children safe," Anya said firmly. "More than once. Now tell me. What did the doctor say?"

Orla dabbed her eyes with a handkerchief. She looked at Anya. "That man," she began.

"Liam told me the tea was... not right..."

"The tea was poisoned," Orla said, voice shaking with anger. "He poisoned tea and gave it to you. And then he led you into the woods and..."

Anya held her gaze. "I'm brave enough to hear it, Orla. You're brave enough to tell me. Please. Before Liam comes back with the children."

Orla stared at this little woman, this artiste, this fellow mother, this fellow wife. This friend. Her words rushed out in a torrent. "He tried to have you, Anya. To violate you. He said... he said you agreed. But of course, you couldn't – the doctor said there is no possibility you would have been conscious enough to even know your name just minutes after swallowing that awful brew. He... he had just laid you down but had... had not the chance to do anything when the wolves beset you. The doctor said by then you were nearly dead with sleep. He ran. He was injured, and more brutally by Liam, but he got away."

"The wolves ran after him?" Anya asked.

Orla shook her head. "I... I couldn't say, no one could. But Anya, it was the strangest thing. It was two days until they found you. By all accounts, the doctor said you should have been... might have... succumbed to the cold, or to the poison of the tea. And yet... Anya, they found you in the den. In a cave made of stones. You were warm. There was fur around you on both sides, on the ground, on your clothes. And the coat you wore... there were teeth marks on the coat – on both shoulders."

Anya reached up and touched her shoulder. She felt no pain.

"Only on the coat, Anya," Orla said. "The sheriff believes they dragged you into the den, intending to..." Orla stopped. "But they must have run off."

"Mama!" Nellie burst through the door.

"Slowly, gently!" Liam warned. The baby squealed in his arms, reaching out for Anya. Both children crawled onto the bed, tucking their heads into Anya's shoulders. No pain, not even a twinge. She kissed them and murmured into their hair. Mrs. Conorach quietly took her leave of the room and went down to the hearth to warm the broth and butter the bread.

When Liam brought the children down, Mrs. Conorach made her way back up the stairs with a tray. She laid a large napkin in Anya's lap before placing they tray on the bed.

Anya looked at her. "Where is he?" she asked.

"On a boat. Back to his wife and child. In Canada." Orla said.

"His wife?" Anya asked. Orla waited, letting Anya absorb this news. "He said she died," Anya said. "In childbirth."

"His wife wrote to the Mayor. Pleading abandonment. The county asked to extradite him back to Canada. To spare his life." Anya stared at her. "Your husband nearly beat him to death, Anya. My husband joined him. And that was before anyone knew the full story."

Anya let out a shuddering breath.

Orla stood, clapping her hands on her skirt. "It's best that he's gone. He won't be let back into the country, much less the town. When there's a poison, Anya, it's best to draw it out for good." She took a small napkin from the tray and dabbed the tears from Anya's face. "When you are feeling better, Mrs. Leighton, perhaps I could ask a favor of you?"

"Anything," Anya said.

"These stitches are not embroidery," Orla said. "They are art. Perhaps you could teach me? I know several of our friends who would like to learn as well."

"There are many things I could teach you," Anya said.

Orla smiled. "Well, we would like to learn. Many of us need more from life than cookery and housework. Who can tell, we may have some artists among us. Like you." She smiled handed Anya the spoon. "When you have taken care of yourself first, my dear. Then you can come to us."

CHAPTER SIXTY-TWO

Liam Leighton, Master Builder. Spirit Stone – Granite.

Shannon Ayers turned the pages of the book slowly until she found what she was looking for.

Granite – protection, abundance, strength. A stone of diplomacy. Use to envision the bigger picture.

Shannon walked to the shelf and brought down the carved box. She opened the lid and took out the double strand of pearls, fastening them around her neck. Their coolness made her shiver. The last days of sunlight filtered through the window of Cairn Cottage and caught the silver edge of the pendant in the box. Shannon lifted that too and walked to the windowsill, holding it to the light. The red jasper stone was broken down the middle, but someone long ago had reset it, filling the cracked piece with solid gold. Gently, she placed it back in the box and shut the lid.

Setting the box on the bureau, she glanced in the mirror, the pearls sending their glow to her face, causing the happy rosiness in her cheeks to shine further.

She knew she didn't look like her grandmother. If anything, her features favored her grandfather. She looked in the mirror and saw Liam's big, wideset eyes, his full lips. Her hand went to her throat to touch the pearls. Did she have her grandmother's strength, though? Her bravery? Her quiet, fierce, patient love?

A baby howled in the cradle in the corner. Shannon glanced over to see the little arms push their way out of the embroidered coverlet, reaching out for comfort, for sustenance, for the change to make their way in the world.

Shannon smiled in the mirror, bowing her head to all the people she saw there, all the people who went before her. All the people who struggled and loved and fought through the world to give her this chance on this earth. She bowed to the Spirit who lived in them all, who drew a line through all that had passed, and all that was to come.

Then she raised her eyes and walked over to the baby wrapped in old yellow silk. She reached her arms into the cradle and lifted up the future.

THE END

ACKNOWLEDGEMENTS

This book is about what it means to embrace your true self; not to fight against society's expectations, but to elevate the society and world in which you live. Anya and all her people find happiness only when they allow those around them to see and appreciate the depth and strength of who they truly are.

I would like to thank my editor, Aimé Merizon, for her encouragement, her thoughtfulness, and her brilliant edits on this work. I would also like to thank the cover artist, Nicole Warrington, for her beautiful interpretation of the story and the symbolism. Thank you to all of owners of the brick-and-mortar stores who carry copies of my debut novel *The Ripple of Stones*, and have carried me across the finish line for this work with their enthusiasm.

A huge thank you to my readers. I am continually humbled that you give your time and attention to the stories I dream up in my head. I am honored to write for you.

Thank you to my parents, who not only gave me every possible opportunity growing up, but lit the fire I needed to finish this book. To my Mom, Sharon, who always has a listening ear, offers of food and childcare, and line-editing. To my Dad, Dan, who will never allow me to give up on myself or my big crazy dreams.

Thank you to my wonderful friends and their families, who gave me thoughtful advice and opinions whenever I asked, and reassured me when I was down.

Thank you to my amazing family for putting up with my "in-the-zone" moments, my flightiness, my storytelling, and my outward drama as I tried to spin drama on the page. Sophie and Henry, you are more wonderful than anything I could dream up. I'll say again, you are the best creations I have had a hand in making. Adam, thank you for your incredible encouragement, your support, your belief in me, and your love. I don't know what I would do without you.

I would like to acknowledge the women who walked before me: my mother, aunts, grandmothers, great-grandmothers, and the even-greater mothers. You pushed and you yearned and you challenged and you loved and you built and you created. You inspired. You laid the path for all of us.

A special thank you to Nellie Young, my late maternal Great-Grandmother. Nellie's real-life bravery and determination are reflected in many of Anya's fictional decisions. My Great-Grandma Young inspired my second novel *and* taught me to chew with my mouth closed; equally important contributions to life, in my humble opinion.

Lastly, a word to anyone who yearns to tell their story, especially my children and students: Find your voice. Pick up a pen; start typing. Push through the discouraging moments, ask for help, learn about your craft. Be humble. Be **brave**. You deserve to be heard and the world will be a better place when your voice joins the chorus.